BLISS
FULLNESS IN
BLUE

BLISS
FULLNESS IN
BLUE

IAN WILCOX

Library of Congress Control Number:		2020902080
ISBN:	Hardcover	978-1-9845-9351-1
	Softcover	978-1-9845-9350-4
	eBook	978-1-9845-9349-8

Print information available on the last page.

Rev. date: 01/30/2020

To order additional copies of this book, contact:
Xlibris
800-056-3182
www.Xlibrispublishing.co.uk
Orders@Xlibrispublishing.co.uk
808436

A DAY IN THE REALMS OF BEAUTY

To
Andrew Jones
My dear valued friend and awesome poetic Brother

The man may be something different
That I do not care
The man is a living marvel
Of one who chose to dare

The person is a friend of mine
That I'm glad off
The next stage of literature we will see
When of my own shall scoff

Andrew is the yet undiscovered
Though has put some works in print
Check him out for yourself
It will make you think

Things like what you know
Things like what you don't
Things that you are willing to
Things you think you won't

THE INQUIRY

BLISS FULLNESS IN BLUE

To Andrew Jones
My poetic Brother

No matter what you're thinking
No matter what you do
There's a certain sense of comfort
Bliss fullness in blue

The tranquillity of water
The reassurance that is sky
The time to reflect on stuff
Without a reason why

The pause of cause without applause
The step back for oneself
The tranquillity of reality
The boost to ones own health

An hour here or maybe day
Longer if am blessed
The sublime restful time
Away from livings test

Oh how I yearn for it again
Stuck in concrete jungle with limited view
To see again the open spaces
To see again but new

That sense of self abandonment
That sense of being free
That relaxing of the daily constraints
That confine both you and me
Bliss fullness in blue waters
Bliss fullness in blue sky
Bliss fullness in blue horizons
Not you see just why

AN APPLE IN THE ACORN PATCH

Climate change seems so strange
Nothing as do know
The climate is a lottery
One day, different seasons show

Sun and rain then Sun again
While a cold wind does blow
Snow could loom before Noon
Though not yet on show

Deception Moms intention
Mother Nature mean
For given up on forecasts
From them nothing glean

Just take on-board and shall not hoard
No need for panic buying
Mix of Sales and possibly Hale
Things are surely trying

Vegetation in hesitation
Not sure quite what to do
Now am witnessing strange sights
Viewing that's that new

An Apple in the Acorn patch
Would be of no surprise
The way that things are happening
Acceptance would be wise

T-shirt and a thick coat
Tucked Hood and pair of gloves
A pair of well dubbed comfy shoes
Mother Nature can have some shoves
Crankiness in the cranial collection

I am not mad
That's pure perception
Maybe slightly
On reflection
Had a mishap
Did I mention

Some crankiness in the cranial collection

Things are different - That is true
Can't now do what once did do
Guess that somehow gives a clue
Almost but not quite same as you
Sit and stare but don't see
That's a part of new me
Look the same way but have changed
Getting over something strange

Fizz, fizz phut at the start
Plip plop gone came along
Made decision, became a vision
Nothing stops you when think strong
Different yes but the same
Still enjoying the new game
Still old me with still same name
Still avoiding things called Fame

Who needs 'perfect'?
When not known
Who is judge
If not own
Free to think
Yes they are
Near and yonder
Close and far

Me? I just have some crankiness in the cranial collection

JUST MAKE BELIEVE

Never give up
On just what you believe
No never give up
However hard life seems
No matter your disability
Of the affliction you have
Never given up on your dream but make it
A reality

Never give up
On all you do each day
Writing about life
And things seen each day
Faces of people both
The young and the old
All have a life's story
Waiting to be told

Andrew Jones

CLAPHAM JUNCTION
(OR THAT FUNCTION)

Decision, decision, decision
Too young for doing this
Free drinks with an old un
Or possible young kiss
Work function that should attend
Or Nightclub that's so good
One is guaranteed to feed
The other understood

Why do I have to choose
Not ready for this yet
I'm in my prime and world is mine
Grabbing what can get
Clapham Junction or that function
Why both on Saturday night
Misery with pleasantly
Or the chance to fight

Work's okay so they say
Why mix thought out of it
Everyone pretending
None though give a shit
Free drinks but costs the staying
When outside mates are playing
Dress up with the unmentionables
Know just what I'm saying

No 'talent' here is what I fear
Unless someone's brought their Daughter
Yet with the Bloke who thinks it joke
Between us will be slaughter
Clapham Junction come to Croydon
At least that part I miss
Give this doo something new
If you get my gist

FOR NEW PASTURES

The man did gently slip away
With hand held by loving Wife
Was the time when no Master
Had to go for new pastures
Five Two years had been together
In that time were parted never
This time though had no choice
So did slip after did voice

"If you love me please don't cry
When I now have to say Goodbye
For is for short time not forever
Until again we are together
Just am going to pastures new
Something some time all must do
Just gone ahead and this time led
Taking chance to make our bed
Where again we will both lie
Soon my dear so please don't cry"

The Lady choking back her tears
Leant and kissed him so dear
Said to him in reply
As he went with gentle sigh

"Yes I love you so wont cry
For this is not our Goodbye
Yes I'll join you very soon
Will be just like a Honeymoon
Then will never part again
Then neither will feel this pain
For will be joined in new pastures
When only good things are our Masters"

FEAST AND FULFILMENT

Join me on this bro I say
For together let words play

Feast, and your halls are crowded,
Succeed and give, and it you live
But no man can help you die,
There is room in the halls of pleasure
For a large and lordly train,
But one by one we must all file on
Through the narrow aisles of pain

Laugh, and the world laughs with you,
Weep, and you weep alone,
The sad old earth must borrow its mirth,
But has trouble enough of it own.
Sing, and the hills will answer,
Sigh, it is lost on the air,
The echoes bound to a joyful sound,
But shrink from voicing care.

Rejoice, and men will seek you,
Grieve, and they turn and go,
They want full measure of all your pleasure,
But they do not need your woe,
Be glad, and your friends are many,
Be sad, and you lose them all,
There are none to decline your nectar wine
But alone you must drink life's gall.

Delectation normal situation
When you know it's right
Love it grows when one knows
Is more than what's on sight
Revelry and frivolity
In a different form
Deeper still that the will
To make the new thing born

Physical or literal
Paper or a creature
One is just as important as other
When in Life does feature
Celebrate when can relate
A commitment sealing pact
A ceremony that some might see
Yet means so more in fact

Bose Enduwe Adogah and Ian Wilcox

FEATURED FRONT AND CENTRE

The Beauty pageant was held each year
Young, aspiring, duly enter
Then one year it had a mind blow
When someone came front and centre
Not the normal stuff of view
They were something that is true
On Wheelchair did rest shoe
They had not much else could do

Yet they were beautiful in who were
They had style and so concur
The panel of judges there in front
The Wheelchair electric so no need for shunt
The one way open, beautiful
The one responded to a call
The one determined that is all
In their dream they could not fall

Featured front and centre
The 'cripple' who dared to enter
For was just being what they be
The rest my friend is history
Changed the rules within rulebook
Changed opinions and outlook
Sure the 'normal' they were shook
When decision just one took

From that day things did change
Other types were not so strange
Point of view they rearrange
When the Wheelchair Queen got her Crown

JOURNEY OF NO RETURN

I find it hard to accept you are not here
For the first time in a life time, I really miss you.

I held your hand as you slipped away.
There would be no coming back from your journey.

I will just have to stay, till I receive my invitation.
To join you in that place of no return.
When we meet up together it will be joyous

Happy day, happy day, happy day.

For now I find it hard to accept you are not here,
Where you are now, you are happy, no tears and at last pain free.
I cannot wish you back that would be very unfair of me.

Happy days, Happy days, happy days.

Penny Wobbly

I AM NOT PERFECT
OR EVEN CLOSE

I have my little foibles
My traits that don't relate
I am a being that you love
I am one you can hate
I am misunderstood so many times
I am understood when deep
I am the writer of some words
Those others choose to keep

I am not perfect or even close
I am just what I am
I will try to justify
Yet quite frankly give no damn
I am normal in the abnormal
I judge with careful care
I am a nothing in world of somethings
Yet I choose to dare

I am a Human being
Just like those this does read
I am multi cultural
With partner of different breed
I am nothing yet am something
I am a spoken voice
Of what can be without insanity
I did make the choice

I am you, perhaps in Blue
Maybe even red
I am just the thing that lurks
Deep inside your head
Look at me with clarity
Look at me with thought
Look at me with sincerity
Now do take a pause

I am me yet am you
Doing nothing you wouldn't do
I am just a Beacon made
For a grander big Parade
Welcome you to Carnival
Greetings so warm send
Let's walk together you and I
Let's help a sick place mend

Not through me for Destiny
Says I am not the cure
I am but a part of it
Yet it needs so much more
Join with me for in reality
We need all to follow
The simple fact to stay intact
Certain prejudice we must swallow

Not those of blatant wrong
That's a decision far too strong
Discrimination as not one Nation
Is the start
Simple solved this equation
By those involved in situation
Not just now but each generation
Contains the seeds of mass elation

I am not perfect or even close
I am me and what you see
But I am a dreamer of big dreams
One day, maybe, reality

FULL UP

Well Full Up Common Kicking
Had enough of that
Guess it all depends where are
The seat on which are sat
Guess what folks I sit on Earth
You do in strange way
So think before you go express
Think before you say

When running drags you down to depths
Lower than did know
When pain you feel cannot seem real
So choose just not to show
Yet show you do for current you
That full of the confusion
More important is distracting
It seems but illusion

Fragrance is so beautiful
When in open air
The mix of many different things
When are forced to share
A colour is but a colour
A shade is but a shade
Yet when combined becomes divine
For a palette made

Yes I am part of palette
Yes I am me still
Yes I am one of many
One of many who until
Say Full Up With Common Kicking
Sick of what I see
Fed up with the ignorance
Yet not ignorant like me

FRIENDS

You once were a stranger.
Then I broke the ice.
We began to talk.
Making conversation.

That fatal "Hello".
Changed everything.
You were an entertainer.
I sure love to listen.
After you performed.
We'd sit and chat.

Never did I imagine
You'd be the friend you are.

Friends are strange people.
There are many different kinds.
Some are tag-alongs.
Not wanting to be left out.

Others are there because
They want to hang out.
Then there's the true friend.
They come running
At any given time.
For any given reason.

There's also Friends
Almost identical to ourselves.
They are tuned right into you.
When we talk, and I'm
Thinking of something.
You out of the blue say
The Words I'm thinking.
No one else has that power.
An ability of your own.

You entertained.
Turned on your wit
You occasionally even show you care.

You have my back.
As I have yours.
I feel I can tell you anything
And know you won't judge.

You too tell me things
Knowing I don't judge.

With understanding,
Laughter and a little love.
You have all the ingredients
To be simply.
My best friend.

Catherine Taylor

WICK WACK HEART ATTACK

Wick Wack Heart attack
So far am I from Home
Another year with hidden tears
Feeling so alone

The numbers drop but they don't stop
Just another one to cross
When am feeling not festive now
As realize what the loss

Just for now this burden Cow
Back again will go
As and when depends on pen
Of Doctor who can show

That all is right for long flight
No problem will I be
Apart from Floating Marbles
That live inside of thee

Clap trap and no back pack
For permanent my goal
Nothing less i confess
Will make me fully whole

A short stay will be play
A move to a planned dream
To be where those who care
Now not impossible seems

Mahal kita Asawa

IS IT SO HARD

The weather today was bad
Not, in truth, the worst had
The days forays shall we say
When were over I was glad

Maudlin in the moment maybe
This and that or just being lazy
Coffee spilt – oops a daisy
Is it so hard to just be me?

To each their own I agree
When they think logically
Not the hatred basically
That's a worry for the free

Upside, downside, inside out
Each is different have no doubt
Some do make want scream and shout
When just try to get about

I love, you love, both love Peace Dove
Different wings though, so it seems
Almost there but not reaching
Mutual sharing of our dreams

Is it so hard to just care
If it this hard then why some dare
To be that foolish to have tried
To show that person are inside

Need support but no-one there
To stand up and say they care
Talk instead to fresh air
Is it so hard? Please tell me not
Nonsense - Good sense

Around an Orange grew a Grape
All is possible if you make
The reader reads what wants to see
That's the fact that's reality
Yet reality is just illusion
When to it add Wordsmith inclusion
Nothing real and nothing's fake
It's just about what of take

The Pomegranate had a summit
With Avocado and Apple too
They decided that divided
Would not be best for mix new
The old ways will still stay
The new just something strange
Yet coexist in harmony
When attitude does change

A joke that is a poem
Not a poem that's a joke
Some may still criticise
At it scorn will poke
Yet evolution is revolution
In some peaceful way
So change adores and then ignore
What the jealous they might say

Tree to air without a care
Spoke as only a Tree can
Rustling and busting
With its branches sang
Thank you for the assistance
Thank you for your addition
Without you I am just a visual
Not that that's my full mission

Nonsense - Good sense? You decide

LODIETA I LOVE YOU

Not supposed to write
The rule set by so many
Give yourself a rest
Before the infinitery
Yet this I have to say
Whatever consequences
We will work this out
Whatever choose the end sequence

Lodieta I love you
More than life itself
Sometimes you drive me crazy
Yet not through chasing wealth
You are the dream I thought just dream
The impossible yet sought
You are the fleeting glance we have
Yet this one somehow caught

Throughout my time many highs and lows
The story of each one
Yet with you a change in me
A promise had begun
You made me focus on the good
Accept then reject the bad
Over all the time together
Realise best I've ever had

Lodieta I love you
In more ways than can tell
By simply being who you are
You cast that special spell
Yes I break a promise
To so many it is true
Yet worth the breaking in my opinion
To say that I love you

Ian Wilcox

ABOMINATION AVARICE

The wiser one, the better one
That who knew and accepted
To gain a place amongst the masses
By one or two must be rejected

The lure was set yet didn't take
Trappings tempting yet didn't bite
Sugar coated for digestion
Yet, somehow, did not feel right

Oh tempting target how you taunt
Glisten brightly and so pure
Extolling virtues so one sided
Fortunately logic cures

False God Fame and sidekick Stardom
Taking more than you do give
I enjoy the peace of nothing
I enjoy this life I live

False fallacies fall you fools
For on stone ground have settled here
Have no wish for your wayward wisdom
Have no thought of failure fear

What will be will surely be
What can choose I will
Nothing ever quite how want it
Yet can cope and do still

The 'cleansing' of the conquered land

Time and again in History
This we read and still see
Yet it should never be
When we get some sanity
Expand a Nation by mutual choices
Learn then earn with other voices
Then one finds that all rejoices
Not the stigma of mass murder

The powerful seek to dominate the weak
Not just help them up
The aggressive message is repulsive
When one has supped from that cup
Yet retribution no solution
When all said and done
Just extending that never ending
Both sides claiming they have won

Look at 'Man' and what we can
Achieve when we try
Fly to the Moon, maybe Mars soon
Yet still some needless die
If not by force from each other
Then from lack of food and cover
When money spent to better kill
Why are others suffering still?

I know the answer I'm afraid
It's part of us and how made
We seem to seek the 'big parade'
Earnt when others of us afraid
When will we learn to get above
That fear is so below a love

P.O.E.T.

There comes a time when things begin
There is a stirring deep within
The need to do something more
The wish to visit foreign shore

Literally or physically
Just the something need to be
The excellence of humanity
Is when, with limits, we can be free

The chance to dance with circumstance
The freedom to just feel
The excitement of the previous extreme
The knowing that you are real

Boy to lad and then to Dad
A journey am still on
Yet with every step stronger get
When realise that I belong

Belong to something bigger
This misfit, sometimes sinner
Realise I was beginner
In something I could be winner

Not of everything just myself
When adapted to different health
The old me went on the shelf
A memory and nothing more

Proud Of Everything Tried
To say not would have lied
Though have no sense of pride
Just satisfaction deep inside

Are you Proud Of Everything Tried
In life and in whatever do
For truth be told if I may be so bold
They are all the making of you

Everything accomplished
Every mistake that each have made
Joined into the person now
So to each a Thanks was bade

Promise Only Evolves True
With each thing we try to do
Some repetition for perfection
Some for have no clue

A whim or flight of fancy
Curiosity or dare
We enter into that unknown
Then results we share

I am a breathing P.O.E.T.
At least I try to be
My life is fuller than could be
Just this side of sanity

I LOVE

I love to wake up in the morning,
To turn gently to see if you are close.
Settling to watch your breathing,
Your face well known and loved sleeping in repose.
The years we have shared together flash before my eyes,
Bringing smiles, a firm grip on laughter as memories float by.
I am trying to fix this moment permanently in my mind.
As age is moving us forward unknowingly.
Towards the end of our truly loving time.
A flicker of eyelashes indicate you are waking,
I wait a moment longer, before greeting and gently kissing you.
The man I love.

DAWNING OF THE DAY

As dawn, slips it's way up over the hill.
So does the old day, slide reluctantly away.
Taking with it the past to be remembered as history.
The birds welcome the dawn of the new day with a song,
With its stories yet to be written and told.
I take pleasure to be here to enjoy it all.

Penny Wobbly of WobblingPen

I CHOSE A DIFFERENT PATH

I shall be telling this with a sigh
Somewhere ages and ages hence,
Two roads diverged in a wood,
And I took the one less travelled by,
And that has made all the difference.

Then took the other, as just as fair,
And having perhaps the better chain,
Because it has was grassy and wanted wear,
Though as for that the passing there
Had worn them really about the same.

Two roads diverged in in yellow wood
And sorry I could not travel both
And be one traveller, long I stood
And looked down one as far as I could
To where it bent in the undergrowth.

And both that morning equally lay
In leaves no step had trodden black,
Oh, I kept the first for another day,
I doubt if should ever come back.

Bose Enduwe Adogah

I HEARD ECHOES

A cold damp morning where am at
A cold emptiness as am sat
A place that really don't want to be
For want to be there with Family
A quiet moment of contemplation
Analysing situation
Stark outside and within
The mood does match - where begin?

Then I heard echoes of the past
I heard something meant to last
I heard voices meant to be
I heard both, both you and me
I heard fortune, I heard Fate
I heard that with which relate
I heard future, I heard joy
I heard that I can employ

Not quite there but getting there
Not quite finished but a start
Not complete but am better
When am thinking with my heart
The ones that make everything worth it
The ones that give me vision
The ones that are a target
The ones that are my mission

To hold again and to kiss
To show each of them how did miss
When separated but not forever
When circumstances made not together

Then I heard echoes of the past
I heard something meant to last
I heard voices meant to be
I heard both, both you and me
I heard fortune, I heard Fate
I heard that with which relate
I heard future, I heard joy
I heard that I can employ
Then I heard echoes of the past
I heard something meant to last
I heard voices meant to be
I heard both, both you and me
I heard fortune, I heard Fate
I heard that with which relate
I heard future, I heard joy
I heard that I can employ

Then I felt much better

SYRUP IN THE SEA OF SANITY

Anxiety or revelation
Queer as folk is this sensation
Caught betwixt and between
Never really sure what means

Making mind up or sit on fence
Go for broke or fear recompense
Highs and lows, fast and slows
Sometimes hidden, sometimes shows

In or out, stay quiet – shout
Never predicting what's about
Only one thing guaranteed
Will rise higher or sink to knees

Going crazy or crazy glad
The worst or best time ever had
Most somewhere just in the middle
As with logic we then fiddle

What more can life throw my way
Thank you so much where can pay?
Up and down and around
Sooner or later on firm ground

Syrup in the sea of sanity
Can be a blessing or calamity
Changing views of that did know
Making journey where should not go

Organisms in an Organisation

Illusion and confusion
Distraction by retraction
Live and learn but above all earn
Judged by Bank balances not action

Techno world so absurd
Manipulating or plain hacked
The world in which nothing real
Stark but simple fact

Reliance is compliance
Why change the things that work
Everything that is 'normal'
To us old timers is berserk

We remember cold hard facts
We remember truth
Does this make us some old relic
When demanding proof

Organisms in an Organisation
The thing that we've become
Ostracised and polarised
When say that am not one

Not too late to correct our fate
Just a chance of thinking
For one self for mutual health
As morning beverage one is drinking

Following rules for that is cool
Just change what do at Home
Let's just see when thought runs free
Allow oneself to roam

Ian Wilcox

TODAY

What will today bring?
Will it be better then yesterday?
Maybe tomorrow will be worth
Hanging around for.

Today is my last day.
That's how I look at it.
Never sure if I'll survive.
Going to give my very best.

I see something new.
I've never seen before.
It wasn't there in yesterday.
Not even the one before.

Let's take a look at it.
See what I need.
It should come with instructions.
I'll try to work it out.

1. Tear the bag carefully.
2. Add a cup of it to happiness
3. Remove the bag labelled Sad.
4. Empty the one tagged Love
To the Happiness.
Also a cup of Thanks.

What is it going to be.
I really have no idea.
Carefully take it outside.
Place in on the ground.

To all people in the world.
This is to ones I have met.
When you call me up next.
Then you say BYE.
As if I'm breathing my very last breath.
I reply my last words to you.
Bye. I LOVE you.

This I say last for a reason.
For if tomorrow comes
And I'm no longer here.
You will always remember
the very last words from me.
I LOVE you.

Never close a day with an argument.
Always finish it with love.
Will we have another chance.
Just to say I Love You.?
We will never know.

Catherine Taylor

MY PERFECT DAUGHTER

Mj Sumayo

She is intelligent and attentive
Caring in her own way
She is a true warrior in Life
No matter what others say
She is her own person
Growing into that task
She will not shirk a challenge
No matter what the ask

She cries when she feels hurt
Laugh when feeling glad
She is an idea gift to me
One of the best I've ever had
She to me is perfect
She has no unseen flaws
She has her 'quiet moments'
Though each they have a cause

Far from me in reality
Yet close in Heart and screen
That for now is enough
To tell her what I mean
When I say that she's the perfect Daughter
No disputing just plain fact
She to me is everything
With every single act

No matter what she will do in life
Nor the flood of tears
I will be here for support
To help ease the fears
She is my awesome Daughter
I think that you now know
She is a part from the one I love
That continues to grow and grow

SAND DOES SOMETIMES

Dad and Daughter spoke at length
One was full of woe
Had first one then came undone
As first did choose to go
One did listen as one did cry
One had been there
One knew why

One simply said

Sand does sometimes soak up sadness
Leaving room for next found gladness
Have a walk upon a Beach
For the start of new to reach
Sand of time and sand not mine
Sand it flows through hand
Trickles fickle and maybe tickles
Yet is just what it is
As does flow experience grows
Less that hurt and misses

Mom and Son sat together
On the porch despite the weather
One thought finding love together
Was a dream that would be never
One did smile to reassure
Knowing what might help cure
What might help move on

One simply said

Sand does sometimes soak up sadness
Leaving room for next found gladness
Have a walk upon a Beach
For the start of new to reach
Sand of time and sand not mine
Sand it flows through hand
Trickles fickle and maybe tickles
Yet is just what it is
As does flow experience grows
Less that hurt and miss

WISHING WONDERS
IN WORLD OF WOE

A world in chaos so it seems
A vision far removed from dreams
A nightmare scenario of own making
Now the results we are taking

More 'intelligent' but more belligerent
Protesting now not 'cool'
Violence a circumstance
Which one then the fool?

Social media the main brain feeder
Not what is outside
Wrapped and trapped as self is sapped
When in screen we hide

Dark outside as angst do hide
Each and every morn
How come to this - the haters kiss?
So different from when were born

Hate myself for addressing
If that I could hate
So despair with a care
That's something can contemplate

Sitting here in silent fear
Of where from here we go
Honestly have no cause to be
Positive with what's on show

Still not too late to change it
Turn aa wrong to right
Wishing wonders in world of woe
Make the future bright

UMBRELLA UP AND PAPER CUP

The weather is abysmal
Nothing new right here
Shortest day the experts say
Christmas drawing near

Stuck in the queue that's growing
Irritation with some showing
Not knowing when transport flowing
No festive mood is sowing

With umbrella up and paper cup
At least the coffee good
Made mistake when journey make
That now understood

Prams are dams in sea of shoppers
Octopuses need to be
When have bags to carry
That go way past three

Panic in the High street
Some have left so late
Choice or just circumstance
Rash buying now their fate

Me, I stuck in queue
Not for shopping but that new
Going to a place again
For a check on a new pain

The roads are getting a free wash
Birds have disappeared
Oversized shelters seem the fashion
Golf type is to be feared
Carbuncle on a crusty creature

We are all one when said and done
Our common denominator is simply one
Yes we all have our pride
Yet under one name we all hide

Boy does that creature need tough skin

Ever changing – growing and shrinking
Peaks and troughs – rising and sinking
Achieve a lot and throw away
A two legged version of Night and Day

With everything in between

Left and right – Love and fight
On an Earth of which can't see
For too big in reality
Though we are making smaller

With it we spread our violence further

We create but cannot relate
We become more lazy
We seek the node to self implore
We are calculated crazy

At last something we seem to be good at

I am a carbuncle on a crusty creature
A claim to fame or redeeming feature
I buck a trend and try to mend
Who out there will support lend?

I could use all the support I can get
Just parades

Accolades are just parades
If bask when do receive
Limiting you in what can do
What you can achieve

Fancy dressing for impressing
Says more about who are
Material not emotional
As drive that new flash car

Seen at places with famous faces
Made none a greater being
Opposite in fact if lack the tact
Of just unfortunately seeing

All for show and don't we know
When image is just wrong
Personality is what we be
Separates us from the throne

Look what made! Just parade
Window dressing if you wish
Yet is not me for you see
I am a nervous dish

Lack the confidence to be myself
To impress I need to try
For I am not that wonderful
Though know no reason why

Now are you thinking about this and yourself??

SOUNDTRACK TO THE SENSE OF SOMETHING

Might be here or might be there
Might affect you, might not care
May be little, maybe not
May be the best or worst thing got

Could be visible, could be heard
Could be logical or absurd
Possibly change a life for good or bad
Possibly make euphoric, possibly deeply sad

A twitch, a twinge, shivers might
Beautifully startle or cause fright
Want to distance or want near
Cause a smile or cause a tear

Self induced or from outside
Grows or shrinks sense of self Pride
Long remembered/ soon forgot
Hits like Petal or gunshot

Old or young, whatever sex
All alike each one gets
Clever/ stupid, quick and slow
Swing the type to and fro

Some leave gasping, some leave puffing
Soundtrack to the sense of something
Is it sixths sense, built in survival
Is it logic or its rival

We will never know what it is but we know that it exists

WHAT WENT WHERE

The couple met again in evening
Shock did meet his Bride
What had had a busy day
The results she couldn't hide

Bag and box aplenty
One corner fully took
Shock went into deep breathing
With a simple look

"What went where?
Why What went?
What went where aplenty
Just how much has What spent?"

"Shock, my dear, don't get excited
Blood pressure already high
Shopping is a part of marriage
So decided I must try"

Shock became dumbfounded
No retort he could then find
True none understand the Female
Unless are one of kind

Argument disguised as Parliament
Or a quiet night instead
Thinking was so easy
Decision promptly said

"Okay my love I commend
Because other choice mad would send
Just warn me in the future please
A sure cure for apoplexy"
A clamp down
(Him and Her)

A clamp down on Chlamydia
What's to fear from being wise
Random actions it's attraction
Is that really such surprise?

A clamp down on impromptu violence
Oral, physical - who gives a toss
When degradation leads to separation
No one wins, each has loss

A clamp down on multimedia
For replacing social meeting
Whilst enjoy that what can employ
Cannot beat a physical greeting

Well screw the world and some who in it
I am thick so am sound
Yet do witness abuse of 'status'
That is galling and profound

A clamp down on the gaming craze
Kill and conquer with just reset
Breeding thought that violence is harmless
No true fact of what can get

A clamp down on intolerance
For others whose alike but not
Apart from those who take it further
To them the ultimate of what got

A clamp down on the attitude
We are better for have earned
Yet all we've learned is ignorance
Teachings are a lesson spurned

And so one sat in middle years
Conquered some then found new fears
Older, wiser has become
Seeing new ways to become undone

Which is right and which is wrong
A maybe lyric for a song
Yet that's all and not much more
If for a future we explore

A clamp down on what is now
A release of what can be
If we just looked beyond the false hope
Everything being technology

Yes enhances yet not replaces
The beauty of seeing real life faces
Getting to know one on one
Is where this journey in truth begun

Begun then stalled as got complacent
Found other things as a replacement
Slowly retarding blissfully disregarding
The joys of moments in fresh air spent

A clamp down on the comfy seats
A clamp down on the ways to advertise
The things appealing yet not essential
Mix and match to them wise

A CLAMP DOWN

You are never completely on your own.
No one on this earth is.
Everyone is tied, and shares connections with others.
That's why humans can never be completely free. It is the
reason that humans feel joy and sorrow. And also love.

There are many unusual thing in this world. Everyday events occur
that cannot be explained, Bizarre Phenomena that often go unnoticed
because people close their eyes to what they don't understand.
But the truth of the matter is, there are many unnoticed things in
the world. And people.... People are the mysterious of them all.

Somedays your heart will rage with fire and some days it
will be numb, clamped with ashes of remains till the end of
the possibility that perhaps it was never present at all.

Life is amazing
And then its awful
And in between the amazing and awful
It's ordinary and mundane and routine
Breath in the amazing
Hold on through the awful and relax and exhale during the ordinary.
That's just living heart-breaking.
Soul-healing, amazing, awful, ordinary life.
And it's breath-takingly beautiful.

If you love something, love it completely
Cherish it, say it but most importantly show it, life is fragile,
and just because something is there one day, it might not
be the next. Never take that for granted. Say what you need
to say, then say a little more, say too much. Love too much.
Everything is temporary but love, love outlives us all.

A clamp down on the ridiculous
The self importance and the hate
A clamp down on the perversity
Before we seal our fate

A clamp down from both sexes
Both sides of what's just one
A tightening of our morale's
Around the Earth begun

Ian Wilcox and Bose Enduwe Adogah

ELEVENSES

(and not in morning)

Sun has gone and young have fun
Judging by the noise
It's ok to make hay
If the supplier others employ
Eleven here but not as near
As where I do belong
Far away from this damned hay
Should turn this into song

'Sober Rover over
Mission control can you still read?
I am sifting through the memories
Can you a future feed?'
The pleasantries of older age
Listening to the young
Doing what was once capable of
Before responsibilities begun

As I sit here with my Caffeine
Guess you'll need yours tomorrow
Make it last this blissful blast
For soon you'll pay in sorrow
Not permanently for you see
Tomorrow do the same
Friday night so it's alright
To on Saturday play again

Cheers you drunken happy fools!!

Am I here again

Am I here again my friend?
Not sure the how or why
Oh well, let's just see what happens
As another few moments they slip by

Pen in hand and open mind
All is good when words find
Never knowing what is growing
Might be something that's worth showing

Could be deep that inside seep
Could be a nonsense true
Could be anything for have not written
Just another Marble smitten

Smitten with the chance so took
Might end up in another Book
So did leak at end of week
As some immortality it does seek

What, in truth, is Poetry
Varies like both you and me
Can it be what wants to be
From meaningful to plain crazy

Never know until one tries
As find are writing with surprise
Just being honest with no guise
Not from trying this one shies

Now were to go I don't know
Maybe round the bend
Better still a sanity pill
Let this one just end

Raising reason into real

So many reasons not to try
So many things do then pass by
So many excuses to not try
Only you know reason why

We all have a 'comfort zone'
A place inside that we do own
Is not public, nor is shown
For too many will condone

Yet what if that does sell us short
What if lethargy one gets caught
Become a one of different sort
Not making most of what's been taught

Waste of space to Human race
When so easy to replace
Just a number, not a face
In some boring losers place

Self religion a decision
That in ourselves believe
Then and only then
Can a mortal more achieve

Nothing set when one gets on
Everything is just bygone
New ambitious to be won
Slowly fear it comes undone
That is fact
That's appeal
The thing that drives
Raising reason into real

SHALL I WEAR GREY

The one did walk about their business
Wrapped in the personal thing
Distraction by attraction
That social media it did bring
Flitting eyes with no surprise
As finger tapped the screen
Concentration not on situation
Nor the problems it could bring

'Shall I wear grey to match the day
Or bright to match my mood
For I am not one for negativity
I think that understood
Yes, pastel colours as a 'medium'
Don't want to be a decoration
For walking past those who this won't last
Because of situation'

The thinking drifting into later
A social gathering to attend
Dress code 'casual' yet slightly formal
Had worries would offend
Amongst the list of things to do
High did this one place
Work was pretty standard
This is more of 'face'

'Shall I wear grey and just blend
Shall I wear something bright
Shall I be another nonentity
Shall I be a sight
Shall I be proud to stand out loud
Shall I just merge in
Is a certain amount of confidence
Admirable or sin?'
Who knows what they wore

ADVANCE YOU ANCIENT

One was lost from what one knew
Ione was back to where one grew
One made choice to see it through
One just did what some might do

One stuck fast to some past
More recent than the old
One so strange completely changed
Another story maybe told

One took a chance and then circumstance
Strangely it did change
All adapted and interacted
To a new life strange

One made the most to lay the ghost
One put things to bed
One moved on became quite strong
Of that which left unsaid

One took the strife and found new life
One did not look back
On did go to others show
What's possible if don't lack

The will to kill attitude still
The strength to prove them wrong
A case in point is 'their joint'
Where fit in so belong

Advance you ancient thin it seems
Advance you chaser by all means
Advance you determined to fulfil
Advance you changed but soldier still

IN A TALENT NOW
ARE CAUGHT

(So many different people I know)

The day was like almost every other
Wake, shower, work, come Home again
Cycling down into Will numbing
Then the one did change the Game
Took a pleasure done for leisure
Gave it focus as were taught
Discovered that others liked their efforts
In a talent now are caught

They benefit from the satisfaction
Others benefit because they do
They are a ray amongst that gloomy
They are refreshing – something new
Playing senses deeply buried
Tugging at things undiscovered
For existed yet so hidden
Amongst repetition deeply covered

Not any more

Now a single soul does change that
Single yes but not alone
For is in the singularity becomes the Nation
Look around and see what's shown
Everybody has a talent
As diverse as molecules
Each acceptable to further test them
If stay within some basic rules

An avalanche starts with one movement
Not all, however, are natural woe
For good can come if and when begun
Within do treat as friend not foe

EVERYTHING FOR REASON

Got limited sight but that's alright
Gave a chance to see
The other side that most try to hide
Yet is in fact a reality
Got to go to that not show
To those unlike their own
The world unheard by fit unserved
By Life in all it's commutations

Been one of those as past shows
Not now I do say
Changes made when things played
And boy! They can some cards then lay
After shock just took stock
Adapt then overcome
Funny though when it did show
Not the only one

Sad, forlorn has been and gone
So has the half empty Glass
Half full now and somehow
This attitude will last

ME BEING FREE

I am constrained by certain things
By choice and not by force
My sense of 'obligation'
Willingly of course

My 'Morales' are overriding
Would not want it other way
I am a creature of a habit
I believe in what I say

I may not be free outside the laws
I am not sure if would want to if I could
For Society needs certain Guidelines
That in all are understood

Yet the opportunity for expression
In police yet unique way
To speak with many others
Hear that said and then what say

I, maybe, sometimes disagree with their opinions
Yet relish the fact that they can them express
The difference between virtue and vitriolic
Is each ones 'acid test'

Me being free is ecstasy
For know that not all have that choice
For some it is a cost in life
To merely sspeak with honest voice

I am blessed and so are you
For you can read this with some calm
Imagine if by reading this
You are inviting serious harm?

SILENT SLEEPER

Silent sleeps the soul of Satisfaction
Troubled sleeps the soul of Right
For not all is quite balanced
Within our day and through our night
Silent sleeps the non carer
Of what goes on around their space
Troubled sleeps the one that's worried
About demise of Human's place

Blissfully go those uncaring
Grabbing all to 'justify'
Troubled walk the broader thinking
Questioning the reasons why
Silent sleep those contented
With the everything they've achieved
Hard to sleep when you have nothing
But worlds too busy so not grieved

Silent sleep in a cocoon
Wrapped around with ignorance
Until the day they are replaced
Then will suffer recompense
Troubled sleeps the chance desired
Not politically but of life
A global gathering of equality
Without pain and without strife

Sleep well you other kind from me
For likes of me let you be
The so called 'cream' of our Morales
That in itself Insanity

EVERY NIGHT I LIE AND LIE

The things that we do tell ourselves
To help as got along
The fantasies we believe
To help us get back strong
Every night I lie and lie
In bed and to myself
Telling this broken body
Is in fact in health

Slowly it believes it
Becomes willing to just try
Though it does not speak to Heart
So knows not just why
Every night beneath the covers
I think of and miss
Two fantastic others
They keep my focused, keep me strong
Keep the reason to belong

Every day I try to play
So compos mentis I can stay
Strange I know but is my way
Not sure if I'm succeeding
Another line at a time
This wasting time is no crime
For whilst doing I feel fine
Until the time to start again

One day soon I'll be in tune
Body clock and that on wall
Until then with paper/ pen
Bit by bit I answer call
Write and write as I fight
To keep the hounds away
Hounds of the long time lonely
Waiting for a reunion

NO, NO NEVER

The young squirrel approached the kitten
A mobile shelter from the rain
The face it saw you would adore
Never thought of pain

"Hello you, how do you do?
Forgive me for intrusion
Yet you seem just a nice accepting thing
That look is not illusion

Both are out and that's no doubt
In this wet that is a pain
Can I ask a strange task
Will your discomfort be my gain?

You are tall with space below
Each a sturdy leg
Can I shelter beneath the space
If needed I will beg

The Kitten looked and hesitated
Not sure what it should do
Then it simply did what's right
Feelings gave a clue

"Both are wet yet one need not be
A simple fact that's true
You I'm sure would shelter me
If were smaller just like you

Come and lay beneath me
I will stand as your umbrella
We will both then talk again
When past is this bad weather

CAUGHT CALAMITY

No-one's ever too young/ too old
For standing ground and being bold
Events they deal with as are sold
Creating history to be told

They caught Calamity and changed its tune
Woe a foe that couldn't grow
Joy would come back soon
Never one for feeling down
Despite what at them threw
Looked beyond the current
Looked at something new
Made the grade with price they paid
Sometimes have just to take
The sad bad and loose what had
Just take it and don't break

Many are they not just few
Doing just what could do
Making sapphires out of blue
Proving legends can be true

They caught Calamity and changed its tune
Woe a foe that couldn't grow
Joy would come back soon
Never one for feeling down
Despite what at them threw
Looked beyond the current
Looked at something new

Are the ones that inspire
Are those filled with inner fire
Pulled themselves out of mire
Those the ones to which aspire

THE SUM

The additional to the miserable
Is not I thinking choose
My reality is almost totally
Mine to gain or lose
One desire is to inspire
Those who feel they need
For not all same despite the name
We are of many a breed

It is told in stories old
That long ago in past
That you and me were family
Shame that could not last
Spread afar now we are
Though getting closer once again
So lives the hope that we can cope
Then extermination of all pain

Am I the sum of my creation
A typical example of my Generation
Full of faults like infatuation
Or am I just plain me?
Am I sworn when were born
To carry on despite the storms
Wake each day before the Dawn
Am I really what you see?
Am I just one or something begun
Behind those open eyes
A part of you that has a clue
The part that we call wise

The mathematical unequivocal
Joy should outweigh sorrow
Let's load one side to stem the tide
Make for a bright tomorrow
Then once more when feel sure
We join hand in hand
Unity with harmony
Earth as just one land

All breeds are just the same
Despite appearance game
Groups within one name
Each creature not just tame
Humanity in our theory
Has risen to the top
So let's show might by doing right
Let's make division stop

Multiplication is a sensation
If increasing the good things
The x a kiss in case did miss
With all the warmth it brings
Subtraction is the flat line
Flat line on screen can show
The ceasing of the prospect
The end of hope to grow

Am I the sum of my creation
A typical example of my Generation
Full of faults like infatuation
Or am I just plain me?
Am I sworn when were born
To carry on despite the storms
Wake each day before the Dawn
Am I really what you see?
Am I just one or something begun
Behind those open eyes
A part of you that has a clue
The part that we call wise

A SINGLE LOOK

A single look is all it took
For me to then decide
A single word from you I heard
That I had found my Bride

A single touch that said so much
A smile that filled the Room
How time flew when spent with you
Seemed to pass too soon

The knowledge came that not the same
As that which went before
Some type in past but no wish to last
Yet with you I do adore

And nothing ever can change emotions
Nothing ever can make us part
For do know and try to show
You do own this Heart

Maha kita my precious Angel
Gawin at palaging ay
I admit
In work and love and play

Ian Wilcox to the awesome Lodieta S Jalosjos

KEEPING UP? BECAUSE
I'M CURIOUS

Some slime is purely natural
Some of it man-made
Some a self defence mechanism
Some results of pleasure trade

Cosmic clouds casting cover
In a spectrum not on show
How and why were discovered
How many people of them know

I light a candle and remember
That cruel day one November
The day that you slipped from me
On this world no longer be

To need or not to need
That's a different question
Not the one that follows A
By a certain person I could mention

Silently floating through deep space
Where is a current upon which travel
Riding Light beams could be an answer
There's a challenge to unravel

The pain still fresh as when did hear
Those dreaded words I did fear
Gone for now but not for good
That's a comfort understood

What would happen I am thinking
As stare at walls with coffee sinking
If put a fridge in walk in freezer
Would it too become a sneezer?

Cosmic, cosmos, cosmopolitan
Cosmo linked but different meanings
Why do words insist on baffling
This I utter whilst teeth cleaning

You slipped peacefully they told me
Somehow seemed your style
For had been at peace since known you
Known you for a while

What's the difference between glare and stare
Does its recipient even care
Why exchange when we can share
Who thought up him Dan Dare?

What is space but some vast sea
Can swim through – no gravity
Yet suffocate instead of drown
When no breath we can breathe down

The hours spent are memories
Happy ones it's true
For you lit a spark in me
Just by being you

If left and right fought up and down
Who would know which side did yield
As an afterthought to this
Where would be the Battlefield?

Cosmic clouds still are rolling
Are they floating or much more
When will someone take the trouble
To them admit do adore

How I miss you my special one
How just knowing keeps me strong
For I sense you watching over
Every night and all day long

Keeping up? Because I'm curious
Am I entertaining or making furious
Chopping, changing here and there
Does it intrigue or don't you care

Three in one for a change
Something, at first, very strange
No not really for is true
Writing's playing and play I do

THE GIFT OF DISABILITY

My disability will
Not hold me back
Although I get frustrated
And annoyed with myself
I'll continue to write
From my heart hand
And pen
And right to the point
Just time and time again

I want so badly to
Inspire others to never
Give up

By Andrew J Jones

AUTUMN FOR THOSE AVARICE

The Spring was fun as begun
To build the nest egg based on wealth
Then not knowing nor were showing
The great impact on their health

Summer came and did gain
In what set out to do
Of the rest? Just second best
For did not have a clue

When can be bought it counts for nought
To appreciate must be earned
Then you know that it can grow
Not just replaced when spurned

With high gain comes a pain
Not now but waiting for
The time to call and watch them fall
As lose what they adore

They've been and done, made a sum
They put enjoyment as a risk
Then do fall as do we all
The Autumn of the avarice

Guess the morale of this verse
Never be that so perverse
To fall into age old curse
Believing everything is money

The best times are when have little
Maybe none, that is true
Then inside you can't hide
Exposed and building a real you
Somewhere in the signal

Misinterpreted by that invented
Human error true
Forget about the internet
It's what we just do

Be it one on one
Looking back a twisted fun
Yet when expands to a 'Land'
Something else has just begun

Somewhere in the signal my love
We lost our conversation
Yet unlike others were not bothered
For understand the situation

Hot head led is woe instead
A thing that I abstain
Yet do not treat me as 'soft touch'
I can, when pushed, cause pain

I feel sick in even mention be
For, that in truth, is not me
Was a warrior but no more
Different path I now explore

Words are weapons yet also shield
For which other side does yield
Toss up of it's worth the cost
When in reflection see what's lost

To quote from a famous song by the awesome David Bowie
Shine on you crazy Diamond

TONIGHT I FED

Tonight I fed my friendly Fox
For by doing of free will
No clearing of the debris
When from my bin does steal

It comes near same time every day
Just standing still and stock
For although knows that when shows
It hasn't learnt to knock

I give it some of my Dinner
For to share it seems good Grace
Plus in truth I cannot finish
So seems a shame to waste

Not sure if it's a tod or vixen
Yes looked up names in Nature Book
Look the same in most ways
The other I didn't look

It is getting used to me
Does not run when open door
Maybe one day will get curious
Try to my inner House explore

That I am not sure I want
In fact screw that for a lark
The effort in removing odour
When its territory tries to mark

No I will just stick to feeding it outside
For no wish to have a Pet
Not quite or should be domesticated
So remain semi wild I will let
A different name for same Game

Pagmamahal says my partner
Αγάπη says a friend
Amor is spoken by another
Hubun does start a trend

Ghṛṇātmaka is so often used
Mrziti heard out loud
Odiarea a source of woe
Fuath of which should not be proud

Languages and living
Receiver and the giving
One side says what should do
Other side, nothing new

Ang gugma says another
愛 somewhere new
Renmen spoken softly
Aroha is what should do

Odio a curse of nature
Hata gives a clue
Ódio was common
नफरत until the love shined through

All both sides of same coin
Been so since that day One
Let's ensure the first one more
Less fight and far more fun
Ian Wilcox

THE GIFT OF DISABILITY

My disability will
Not hold me back
Although I get frustrated
And annoyed with myself
I'll continue to write
From my heart hand
And pen
And right to the point
Just time and time again

I want so badly to
Inspire others to never
Give up

By Andrew J Jones

HOBBIT HURTLING HORSEBACK

Life is full of the unexpected
Life is full of unexpected things
Life is full of startling wonders
Life is full of Ropes and Strings
What 'we know' we don't really know
What we don't is often true
So we blag our way through it
If you're honest this is true

I saw a Hobbit hurtling Horseback
To where go I have no clue
For they are truly unfathomable
They just think and so then do
I never knew of their existence
Yes that's true despite my age
Then one day, hip, hip hooray
I found them courtesy of a story page

Not the normal I do grant you
In fact I guess sounds quite absurd
Yet I saw that bouncing creature
Will not repeat the things I heard!
Yet plain as day dawns seven times a week
I am sure of that for have Calendar by my side
Nothing seen quite as serene
As watching that thing try to ride!

Arms and legs akimbo
Yelps I think of joy it did employ
All can say is hope and pray
I hope it was no Boy
Each time did land upon the seat
A new menu it could eat !!
Ian Wilcox

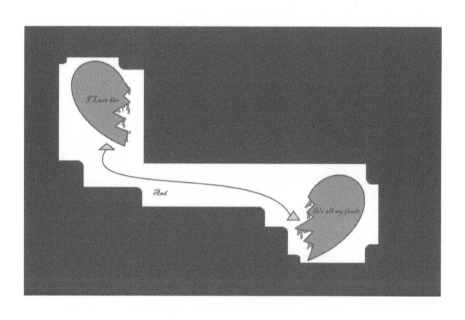

FIRST LOVE LOST

I can't stop thinking of you
I can't stop crying over you
They tell me to move on
So why is it so hard

I drink my problems
I drink my sadness
Sometimes I find myself
Just staring into space and end up crying

You made a promise
A promise that you broke
A promise that you've said
You'd wait and stay but didn't

It broke me
It made me feel a fool
To believe such promises
Most importantly you lied

All I did was to love you
Gave everything that I could gave you
I even chose you
I chose you

I want to be mad at you
I want to yell at you
I want to scream
but I cant

I still end up forgiving you
I cant be mad at you,
I just cant
I think this is love

A love that betrayed me
Yet still loving and forgiving you
For everything
I love you so much

But I have to say goodbye
I have to move on
I know it will take a lot of time to forget you
But I'll try

I love you my love
But also this is a Goodbye

Mj Sumayo

SITUATION A CREATION

Ever had that feeling
Life and World against you
Take a moment to yourself
This is nothing compared to true

You are better than have got
You are you - That means a lot
Who really cares about the others
Unless friendship and family covers

First and foremost you are you
You will do what you will do
If they don't know you have no clue
Even knowing, sometimes true

A situation a creation
When do look in retrospect
For without the push it gave you
Never would that dream you get

Negatives and Positives
Are like the proverbial known Olives
Black and Green yet both mean
The image of the Sun is seen

Shed off despair for that's nowhere
You are going places
Be gone forlorn for new is born
With lots of smiling faces

Ian Wilcox

TO THE ONE THAT HEARS THE MUSIC

The silence is so deafening
The air a morbid state
The mood so rude it is bad food
The present I can't relate
Know not when sense again
Will rise if ever do
That my friend needs a trend
I guess it's up to you

Long before did hate adore
We coexisted without clue
Modern stuff gets most in huff
So much for the new
Attitudes become so rude
When to masses they can shout
Promising the ultimate sin
Whilst in comfort there's no doubt

The drums are beating so no retreating
Unless a Brave does say
Let's not go to what we know
There is a better way

To the one that hears the music
Each beat that they are playing
The one that listens to the vocals
Every word and how are saying
To those who listen but don't judge
Until they listen just once more
To the ones who can take further
When do see the open door

Ian Wilcox

I CAME, I SAW, I KICKED SOME

The old replaced by new
It's just a thing we do
Nothing special in what do
Just a part of growing up

I was to some a wild one
Not understanding my sense of fun
That type of thinking came undone
When I met some others

Others who were if truth be told
So much wiser for were old
Been and done amongst the fold
Of better than I am

I took what said of they lives they'd led
I stored it deep inside my head
Looked at self and then instead
Became a wiser person

I came, I saw, I kicked some ****
Yet that was then, so in the past
That type of thinking not meant to last
As we grow we move on

Now am content with time I spent
But that is so old me
As I grew then I knew
Life's for living not frivolously

IF EVER WAS NEVER, JUST FOREVER

If ever was never, just forever
Would Mankind start again
If a no show to somewhere go
Would we continue to be this pain?

Snowdrops out of season
Bloom for no real reason
Beautiful they still be
When a glimpse of them can see

Why the right to hate on sight
That which is not known
When in reality it could be
Glorious when it is shown

Dandelions dancing in the dark
Away from prying eyes
Choosing partner subtly
Before telling Bees with added spice

Could the good remove the hood
That veils a blinkered vision
Sow then grow the way to go
Instead of superstition

Carnations are salvation
When flourish in the fields
Worn when sworn to new life born
With everything it yields

Which way is the right way
When at crossroads one does stand
Depending on how you think
Maybe foreign lands

NOW'S THE TIME

Lodieta ang nawawalang piraso ko

Time ticks by for you and I
Side by side forever
Where will go no-one knows
Yet go we will together

You gave me security
You gave a Family
You gave me one that shines like Sun
You gave me hope and pride

You gave and then keep giving
You make a life worth living
You both are there so I don't care
For my love has perfect pair

You answered questions that I sought
When over oceans one I caught
Though yourself had things quite fraught
Still accepted ring I bought

So now's the time I must confess
So my conscience then can rest
You give me no second best
When answering question with a yes

You made me see what could be
You showed a new way true
You did and do something new
Just because you love as i love you

CARMINA BURANA

Mind-set meltdown causes full frown
Not a path I wish to choose
Being free is totally me
A thing no wish to lose

I maybe crazy but am not lazy
At least with use of pen
They sound absurd when from others heard
Every now and then when

Fiction is a friction
Fact a simple act
The words go to where know
Sanity is half intact

"Excuse me Miss by why have
That Goblin cooking meal?
My desire is to inquire
What when shake hands you feel?"

Insanity may be free
If compared to money cost
Yet is dear when you fear
Everything that's lost

One more show before I go
To someplace that's somewhere
The sad truth is found in proof
By my disconcerting stare

Did anyone else see that flying Trifle?

WANDERING WISTFULLY
WITHOUT SUNLIGHT

Sometimes you need a moment
Sometimes you need some space
Sometimes want some solitude
Away from that you face

When attraction becomes distraction
Something else is sought
A breakaway from crazy day
Before in another caught

So the time just feels fine
Shared with the unspoken, but not few
Moon and electric light, now new bulbs and so, so bright
An option that can do

The beautiful peace of the release
The comfort within the solitude
Not much chance of hateful glance
Of day walkers sometimes rude

Sharing streets with natures feats
The nocturnal that slip by
No conversation for from different nations
Understanding so know why

Preparing for the sharing
Of those yet to awake
Wandering wistfully without sunlight
A chance one likes to take

THE ARGOS OF THE AFFILIATE ABSTAINER

To many 'almost' but not quite you
They share just something that you do
Sometimes wise to compromise
Sometimes best to walk away

Both have risks in their decision
Think carefully before submission
Lauded or some plain derision
Either way you never win

Argos – the city that sat on fence
Fell foul of all because of that
Maybe what it lacked the problem
For that thing was what we call tact

To abstain can be a pain
Yet affiliation likewise true
Courage needed in conviction
At end of day do best do

Best for you to sleep easy
Best for you to carry on
Best for you in the long run
When make decision there is no wrong

Some maybe could be better
With the gift of hindsight
Yet the fact that you made one
Meant in someway it was right

Oi ischyroí épesan se kairó, o kathénas eíche énan lógo gia ton opoío
The mighty fell in times gone by yet each had a reason why

Ian Wilcox

WATCHING WATER WANDER WAYWARD

Walked past a stream that fed a river
River met a big expanse
Time it took for the journey
To reflect gave a chance
Taken for granted will be there
Thought of absent we don't dare
Yet the cycle is a marvel
As upon that fluid I now stare

Reflection is perception
If we but just slow down
Mysteries are complexities
What really wears the Crown?
Us or it that upon which sit
That we just take for granted
Yet in truth we are aloof
Infact we are enchanted

Waiting water wander wayward
Wondering how many times before
Touching occasionally a river/ stream bank
Or stuck in midst/ lap on shore
Up and down a recycling
Thing not seen until seen
Vapours/ solids or at least liquids
How many places has it been?

As air we breathe we do deceive
We are the thing superior
Yet true is told we cannot hold
A Candle when inferior
Yes we can change physical
To adapt it for our means
That is not life as we call

Ian Wilcox

10 MINUTES

Ten minutes here, ten minutes there
The most at which a screen now stare
Not so bad in wide scheme of things
When can still see what disaster brings
To others that are across the Globe
That have to find that thing called Hope
Yet they do and battle through
With integrity they still cope

So ten minutes here and ten minutes there
The chance to which some diatribe share
Not really a problem being
With lack of that we know as seeing
Not at top but not at bottom
Been and done and forgotten
Now the chance once again
To try to help and faith regain

Faith in self and not the other
That for other day to cover
If at all for not my call
That I leave to another
Each to own and what is shown
The 'poor' are sometimes wealthy
For what lack in one thing another they bring
Like an attitude that is healthy

10 minute stare here and there
My day is then complete
With those new and friendship grew
With those I've yet to greet

ALL THE SOUNDS

The walk to Park for a lark
The High street bold adventure took
The casual stroll to feel whole
The cover not the Book
That inside prefers to hide
Ironic at its best
When can't see more words than three
That is also test

All the sounds go round and round
They me nothing much to me
For have got the 'job lot'
From who with meant to be
The noise outside is mere pride
If taken for just granted
When you know it soon goes
If to one are enchanted

Vision was a mission
Part achieved it's true
Yet is more so can endure
After what went through
No sight is blight
Like permanent night
The darkness so depressing
So back some got and means a lot
A sign I am progressing

All the sounds go round and round
Within a single Head
Not that much more need for sure
When found them whom I adore

BLOODSHOT EYES

Bloodshot eyes and not so wise
The pen has gone berserk
When ideas come it is just fun
Writers don't class it as work

Another page to quell the rage
To complete the story see
Be it be fact or, maybe, fiction
Novel or poetry

All Time is right within the plight
No clock to thinking known
Be it dark? That's lightbulbs lark
For making the ink shown

Insomniacs just for cracks
The target almost reached
Another one and nearly done
This driftwood soon be beached

Coffee yes to help the quest
Caffeine is the rule
Alcohol makes flow slow
That's just for the fool

Of clear Mind is productive kind
Just irrational some might find
When takes over in fields of Clover
The hours are no bind

CARMINA BURANA

Mind-set meltdown causes full frown
Not a path I wish to choose
Being free is totally me
A thing no wish to lose

I maybe crazy but am not lazy
At least with use of pen
They sound absurd when from others heard
Every now and then when

Fiction is a friction
Fact a simple act
The words go to where know
Sanity is half intact

"Excuse me Miss by why have
That Goblin cooking meal?
My desire is to inquire
What when shake hands you feel?"

Insanity may be free
If compared to money cost
Yet is dear when you fear
Everything that's lost

One more show before I go
To someplace that's somewhere
The sad truth is found in proof
By my disconcerting stare

Did anyone else see that flying Trifle?

EVERN CAME

Evern came and did the same
Evern made a choice
In so much silly stuff
Evern had a voice

Spoke with truth and not aloof
Spoke of what I understand
Spoke of unity not disparity
Spoke of one mutual Land

Evern is one I admire
Though to say would make him blush
Evern has some qualities
Just keeps them rather hush

Evern sent and I spent
Time absorbing what received
Yes I know no one trick show
Yet for this one I truly grieved

Evern is a Masterpiece
Beneath a hidden cover
Yet I implore – please look more
For an Evern had a Mother

Evern came in many a name
The choice of which is yours
Evern is a simple man
Though that word could mean both sexes

CLIMATE CLIMBING

Climate climbing will self confidence
The other type of which no sense
This one comes without recompense
When you unlock your own ability

Wealth does soar when not quite adore
Just happy with the one
That you became for all are same
Each just like some fun

You have been down to the darkest places
Yet can still climb back to the top
Just believe that can achieve
Then nothing can or will stop

Climate climbing within one own
Attitude so proudly shown
Been and done but in the past
Being down just didn't last

Natural maybe another feature
Yet is nothing but a Teacher
For something else that we can change
When ourselves we rearrange

Climate climbing first is self
For the benefits of Mental health
Start with this and it is true
Not that much that you can't do

ANOTHER SIP

Another sip or biscuit dip?
Too early yet to think
Day's just changed, numbers rearranged
As first drink I drink

As with sweet I meet to complete
That known as waking process
Blather now like confused Cow
Definitely a work in progress

Not that bright when things are right
So Heavens help when warming up
Multi tasking as break my fasting
Through being a sleep Pup

One more encore eyes implore
Want more closure so it seems
'Hold on you!' says something new
'Had enough of dreams!'

So another sip does pass my lips
As debate continues on
Just wish/ beseech decision reach
Before this liquid's gone!

CRAZINESS IS QUADRANT QUATTRO

N.A.S.A. and others took a look
Then consulted 'the known' book
Nothing like it they could see
In both Human and 'Alien' history

The changes that were taking place
The prospects for them to now face
Turmoil now a mere precursor
To something worse or worser

A different language they did speak
On Earth grammatically not at peak
Yet all irrelevant said and done
When added to the future sum

The 'aliens' are revolting
Not that opinion but the act
Other Quadrant had a pact
The potential was deeply worrying

Stability was history
As far as onlookers saw and 'see'
The reason why were just opinion
When compare to that called minion

A revolution was a solution
So that is what they chose
Not thinking much about such
As the impact of them that were not close

N.A.S.A. sent an urgent message
To the top of the list of things
Others did the same in places
That not so much attention brings

Let's see what happens

CREEPINESS IN
COLD CORNERS

That certain Room
That certain space
Yet looks the same
Yet Heart does race
That certain feeling unexplainable
Yet for your attention it is capable
Nothing logical you are able
To justify this emotion unstable

A 'New build' can still yield
An older one is half expected
Yet the same with different name
Please feel free if need corrected
That certain tingle that isn't Shingles
That sudden feel of cold
That aware of strange stare
Of one as yet untold

Creepiness in cold corners
In the Tropical or colder climes
The freeze of blood that becomes a flood
As wall clock hours chimes
Alone with company but cannot talk
For the just float instead of walk
They are there and do not care
If to them you are aware

SOLOMON SWAM

Solomon swam up to the Dam
Trish just made some Toffee
Candice did please with literary tease
Ian just drank more coffee

Charles with smile did beguile
Sandra liked the sand
Bob had a job that made him 'snob'
Felicia crafted with left Hand

Archie, maybe, slightly crazy
Lorraine was quite the same
Steve had reprieve that was relief
Hondora hated her own name

What's in a name but recognition?
What ever is not you
For when given could not speak
Nor even have a clue

It's how we act and that's a fact
That makes us who we are
We are what be and not just see
We are and no priced car

Malcolm explored the fathoms
Beatrice kept some Bees
Mable considered stable
Ian just drank yet more coffee

COLDER CLIMATES

Colder climates so confusing
When extra heat I find I'm using
Turn it on then off again
Sun goes away then appears with rain

Clear but cold then cloudy wet
When will I this stage can forget
Ritual of where, currently, living
So I guess must be forgiving

Nothing new like shiny shoe
Repetition with a change
Yup it's like that just said
The variations to rearrange

Colder weather half expected
Yet to Body is rejected
Has got used to something new
So despite warnings has no clue

In a quandary so just write
A self confessed luxury blight
I guess there is just one thing to do
Get back to the warmer knew

FULL THROTTLE FUNKY FUN

As one door closes another opens
If to pass through you do choose
Just say 'Hey! What more can pay?'
There's nothing much to lose

So I saw and looked more
Into that statement said
Resonates and dictates
A new way it then led

Out with old and in with new
Let's see what with this can do
Learning new things and what brings
The shocks that one goes now in to

Full throttle funky fun
That's the new one just begun
Different yes and sometimes test
Yet I can still feel Sun

No harm done when become
A better one for the experience
So now fun at what have become
It's really nothing serious

Yup full throttle now a blast
Destination – hey whatever
Better than just moping around
Even if it's not that clever

FURRY FRIENDS

Furry friends now a trend
Once were a mere solution
To aid and made a simple trade
They started 'revolution'

Where one that was just practical
Now become that so emphatically
Own 'pamper stations' now situation
That leaves one quite exhaustible

They take us over with affection
They worry us about rejection
Then become a Family injection
Seemingly without perception

Furry friends that do as please
That are playful or simply tease
'Domesticated' from that 'wild'
Pretty much another child

MUCHAMUDDLED

Muchamuddled – they befuddled
Not that that normal see
A creative in what stated
A blessing unto me

Muchamuddled is so bold
In the things told/ untold
Yet a candle they still hold
To a future might unfold

Muchamuddled badly named
For deep down are just the same
Doing what they think true
Doing what and so can do

Many are the much a muddled
Boundless are those befuddled
All just wish to be cuddled
By someone who understands

NOTHING'S TRUE BUT

The world of spin is in full action
The results attraction/ distraction
Nothing new when opinions chew
But.?....

The things I have are like a salve
So much that I can say
We three known as Family
Are Forever and a day

The world around is so profound
It influences true
We adjust as we must
Just find and then get through

We are not immortal on this thing
Yet eternal in another
Yes each are different in thing called 'look's
Yet same so we don't bother

To think about that insignificant
To think that this is wrong
We all know just what we feel
We all know together we belong

Nothing true but true love
Nothing true but own Family
Nothing true but recognition
Nothing true in what first see

THE ULTIMATE MOTHER

We all have one since we've begun
Yet all do have another
Whilst we live in what she Gives
Nature is the ultimate Mother

We take for granted at our cost
She does scold and things get lost
We are the rebellious child she has
She replies with a blast

How much depends on certain trends
Our willingness to just destroy
With ability comes responsibility
Mother is no toy

And when to late to change our fate
Will we then finally learn
The gift bestowed ae should hold
Not something to just spurn

Many Mothers with different covers
Yet this one stands apart
For many a child both tame and wild
Since each one did start

The ultimate Mother has many another
More children than we know
If understood then know how good
Appreciate her glow

IN THE MEETING

THINGS HAPPEN

They say things happen for a reason.
I believe that's true.
But why so many bad?
Can't we learn from the good?
Are we not capable?

We always remember bad times.
Struggle remembering the good.
Good is to feel happy.
Glad that something went right.
Not to remind us of the sad.

As humans we learn better
From the bad.
Maybe it's to make us grow,
Or teach us to appreciate
What we had and have.

Good times we don't
Recall too well.
We have to think hard about them.
Most times they're a outcome
Arising from something bad.

I guess if there was no bad things,
We'd have no reason,
To appreciate the good times.
They would all be the same.
Learn to appreciate what you have.
Don't take the good for granted.
Remember it can all be taken away
In the blink of an eye.

Catherine Taylor

EPILEPTIC ENTERTAINMENT

I saw spaceships in the ceiling light
In carpet Dolphins swam
The place I sat became Top Hat
My Tablet Boiled Ham
I floated on a strange strong breeze
My body lost control
Shook like I'd been electrocute
Was prone where once I stood

When will end this new found trend
Obtained after 'my adventures'
Post Stroke Epilepsy amongst other things
I choose not now to censure
Written from a vague memory
Before I did pass out
Not then but much later
As my bruises scream and shout

How many will turn to battle scars
How many fade away
Too fresh to know as start to show
Will find out another day
The world I'd seen didn't mean
I wanted it to join
The spasms made as short circuits played
The flipping of a coin

Embarrassment and discontent
When in public places do
Shame to say wont go away
Just becoming thing not new

WHEN WISHES TURN TO WONDER

Not the reason nor that expected
If in all honesty, believed would be rejected
Just a simple soul at heart, not one for the fame
Just encouraging people who are better
That's my simple aim

Life has twists
To promote, it seems, first one needs to be known
That is something out of my control
Only my involvement I do own
I intend to use it

Public appearances will just be me
Doing what others do
Going out for shopping
Joining checkout queue
Just another person

Yes you may see posts on Social media
Advertising wares
That is just spreading the message
To anyone that cares
The message of harmony and unity

Iwi is a normal bloke
Different in certain things
Iwi has some Floating Marbles
Deals with that and brings
Honestly I am not crazy

When wishes turn to wonder
Aghast is what I be
A nothing in a big, big sea
The truth that is me
Motivate and generate – the written word

SHENANIGANS IN SHADY SHANTIES

In my teens I was keen
To obtain what was able
This and that without claptrap
Only doing when was capable

Boy! What a journey that was!

Now grown up and drink from one cup
Looking back don't recognise
The one then that wrote with other pen
With the ink that satisfies

I laugh at old me that wasn't old

How survived when wasn't wise
Still trying to work out
In and out with no doubt
Wondering if would get clout

The joys of immature bravado

Her and her and maybe her
I had needs and them the cure
Nothing there you could call pure
Just an act that could leave sore

Anyone got a recharger?

Ahhhh the old days with those old ways
What the heck was i then thinking!
Not that much above the navel
If truth be told as eyes blinking

Laughing that much that I am crying

FAITH

I have it in us despite the differences

I come from one place, you another
Yet are same - Sister/ Brother
Influences all around
In a Faith find comfort ground

Irrespective of the faith followed
We are all one in the eyes of the creator,
All we need is love
Helping and empowering others is the greatest
gift we can give back to Him

The Creator comes with many different names
Depending from where are
Yet, irrespective, of their distance
Watches over from afar

Irrespective of the faith followed
Destruction is never meant for us
Because we are the gift of the same Holy Spirit
All we need is love to make our dreams come true

Muscle, sinew, flesh and blood
Common to us all
Yet like the difference in appearance
Diverse is the belief call

Different in speaking
Different in learning
Different in tolerating
Different in feelings
Different in worshiping
We are from one creator one God.

Yes God, but who is God?
A collective name I say
Like other things in various places
Various names at play

I guess He made Himself invisible
But I know He lives in you and He lives in everyone.
Only those who loved Him, He manifest Himself to.
His love helps us to help others by empowering them

Following An Instinct To Heal
Faith as a variation
Adapted and at times abused
Sadly this is true

Truly I concur with your thoughts
We are different so is our mind
Our faith are different and believes also
Still we are one entity

To heal not torture
To join not slaughter
To pacify and unify
Surely that's the reason why

You got my point
To strengthen not to intimidate
To encourage not abuse
To help not to downgrade
To serve humanity that's my goal and to unity I stand for

Again I say to whichever pray
We are one beneath our choices
Yes our worship of many things
Is as personal as our voices

A collaboration between Bose Enduwe Adogah and Ian Wilcox

NO PREZZIES CHRISTMAS

Another empty Stocking
For a Christmas day
Not even a Satsuma
Or some of Rudolph's Hay

I am a nasty person
That is purely true
When i can still giggle
At just what did do

I saw him the other year
He came in through the window
Looked at me, looked at his list
Said "Up yours!" and left!

He has never forgiven me I think for the year
That I put chilli powder and sea salt in the Cookies I left out for him
His hat left a dent in the ceiling!!!

He went out faster than came in
As I creased up in my Bed
Rudolph and Team had no need to gallop
As off the sleigh it sped

Since that year it is the same
A record on repeat
Better off buying myself two stockings
Putting on my feet

No Prezzies Christmas I have solved
In a simple way
From day before until day after
Fast asleep I stay

FASCINATION AT
THE IRRITATION

One side shouts the other screams
The first screams just as loud
Discussion lost in volume battle
Logic loses against proud

Sit and listen to Buffoons
Better sometimes than the tunes
Fascination at the irritation
Worse than them with those Sand dunes

Generalising in my surmising
Not all are same that's true
Just come to mind for some of kind
Grab the headlines do

Everyone is always right
That's just how it seems
If only all were right on same thing
That's the stuff of dreams

Diversity and complexity
Are mortality true
Yet why hate when don't relate
The opinions of me and you

Opinion is our given right
Provided peaceful stated
For at end of day come what may
Deep down all are related

Fascination at the irritation
It stirs in some - not all
We all know for History shows
They are the ones that fall

ENEMY OF A STATE (OF MIND)

They've been abusive by being clueless
Change a life with stroke of pen
Then how go when time to show?
Cannot be bothered then

Create a year full of fear
When next will you eat
Nothing much to them such
As themselves they treat

But what of Joe Public?
Those that they affect
What of the ones that need most
Anything that can get?

Nothing much as far as concerned
They are plainly careless for position earned
An enemy of a State (of mind)
You can fight back I have learned

Be persistent, be determined
Brush aside the try to intimidate
Stay true and just charge through
You become the thing they hate

A mere number on a list they see
Nothing Human for cannot be
Just a target to reduce
So a rejection they produce

Until it's taken further

FOUR THIRTY THOUGHT

Acrid the ache of aged aggression
Tranquil turns the tide transition
Peace does play in poverty
Yet ignored by likes of me
Spoilt in our comfort zones
With flash cars and posh homes
Not caring for the one that owns
Not much more than skin and bones

Illiteracy a destiny
For so many in poverty
Just getting by as what be
Not much future do they see
Start to finish, hope not longer
Getting frail instead of stronger
Condemned! Life sentence! Yet no crime
Other than wrong place, wrong time

Modern world, progressive world
World unfurled yet so absurd
When rich prosper and abuse
When land and poorer
They just use
All take no give, no chance to break
The modern cycle we now make
Downward spiral if no care
Part of wealth choose not share

Not the monetary quite as such
Though that would help very much
The things we have as 'higher' nations
The products of our own creations
If we just choose not to lose
Enhance, encourage, abolish factions
Reap the rewards of interactions

Six Thirty and still thinking

Time has flown and my stubbles grown
Yet still grey matter goes
More useless words that maybe heard
Might on someday on paper shows

Soon be time for breakfast
Long distance with the Wife
Her her lunch for ahead
The vagaries of spoon and knife

Plans today? Not quite sure
Nothing much I need to do
Some admin for completion
Of a project I chose the fool

Why does this choose to happen
Random words do want to leak
Force me to pick up the pen
Before the ears do squeak

The mad rush as ink does flush
From one place to another
Poor old plain sheet that was once neat
Now with mess I cover

Not supposed to write to rest my sight
Keep this quiet please
If Wife finds out I'll get a clout
That will drop me to my knees

Eight Thirty, sky is dirty

Eight thirty and sky is dirty
Unless Duck won't be much fun
Wet parade for brolly made
A day off for the Sun

Now a day more complicated
When can't consider going out
Can but too much hassle
All those layers wrapped about

Guess I will have to amuse myself
Yet again this time of year
As counting down to Christmas
All the false frivolity and cheer

If friend I call good fortune
Remembers me this day
Something will happen to occupy me
Whilst better half away

What's going on with my inner clock
Two hours between each glance
Have I some secret metronome
Is it purely chance

Enough of all this claptrap
A notes become a saga
Before you know will be eating junk
Washed down with pint of Lager

Then my woes will REALLY begin!!!

WIW

Hello you - hello you
Are you one or are you two?
Honesty, I have no clue
Imagining the things can do

Only difference is first name
Everything else is the same
Are you playing some strange game
Double exposure in same frame

Twins I've met and that was something
Identical ones- next to nothing
Blooming heck! Even speed!
Just how far does this thing reach?

Please don't move for will confuse
Though to you it would amuse
Just stand still while I choose
Which one in wonder to peruse

You must have been a nightmare
To parents growing up
When one said they were thirsty
Which to give the cup

My eyeballs are in meltdown
Trying to set apart
Can one say name and hold up hand
At least will be a start

Stop switching please just to tease
Your sense of humour's crazy
I am now exhausted
And I am anything but lazy!!

GLOBAL GREETINGS

Global greetings greatly garnish
This strange sphere on which appear
Mind set meetings however fleeting
Brings us closer, draws us near

Search for life on other Planets
Yet do shun that on own
Make amazing vessels for space travel
Yet to own are not full grown

Pause and think about that for a moment

Mock and laugh, want Autograph
Look up to some and down on others
Yet we all are the same
One basic shape covers - smothers

Developed Hands to grasp and hold
Developed speech for thinking told
Developed years to say how old
Developed Trade for bought and sold

Yet some still despise based on looks and choices

Global greetings and warm meetings
If only that could see
The grow together that ends never
What a rich place Earth would be

No hate, no pain, no kill for gain
No persecution and retribution
Replaced with haste welcome face
My fantasy solution

WONKY WALTHER

Wonky Walther thought could walk on water
At least at certain times
Much consumption slowed down function
That various were the crimes
Different drink pushing to the brink
Of upright getting Home
For not the place to sober face
When through death are now alone

Wonky Walther sometimes falters
As staggering he does go
No one left for one bereft
At least none choose to show
A 'semi celebrity' in the neighbourhood
None though choose to aid
They are all too 'busy'
With own choices that they've made

Dishevelled and despondent
Staggered Walther true
To were with dare none did care
Never searching for a clue

Then they found him

The 'old drunk' had finally sunk
To place with no return
On a street where others meet
His reunion he did earn
When blocking path he did at last
Get recognition but too late
Somehow all too common
Poor old Walther's fate

PEACE IN THE HANDS OF LOVE

Great minds over the generations have thought deeply to craft peace
into mankind's care for every living thing who resides on this earth.
They cast their thoughts of care and nurturing
upon the wind to settle seeds everywhere.

Seeds of respect, kindness, love, support, honesty.
Seeds which they hoped would grow and
combine in strength to produce PEACE.
Sadly, mankind needs constant reminders to leave
greed, hate, terror and cruelty behind.

They forget the loss, destruction and mutilation of families
and the end to some blood lines. The loss of homes, food
and water supplies, education and medical services.
Never perhaps in their life time will they witness
a return to life as it once was. You can

Our great minds must again write about
the seeds of PEACE and love.
Allowing them to be carried once more in the
wind to fall into searching minds.
Turning dreadful times into hope, encouraging stability,
regrowth, respect, honesty, sharing and friendship to take over.

In our hands we carry this great responsibility, to by example and courage, spread the word about peaceful living and nurturing for all living creatures that share this planet Earth. No matter how insignificant.
The great minds of the past, write to remind us the future:

To keep the PEACE in The hands of love.

Penny Wobbly

KENDAL MINT CAKE

Middle of nowhere, windswept moor
Wilting fast as self explore
Batteries in the Danger zone
Dig deep in pocket for know what own

That slab of sugar heaven
Disguised with refreshing taste
That instant bolt of energy
None of which will waste

The outdoor survival rations
Many do forget
Based in some English old, old place
When world let us rule - FORGET!!!

That strange texture that is moreish
That Petrol Station that you eat
That mix of breath freshener that rots teeth
As a conundrum hard to beat

I love to eat Kendal mint cake
Yet only when I need
Guess resigned to history
As other stamina I now feed

Not sure about the modern twist
Chocolate coating why not sure
Not something for confectionary
Survival kit and pure

ONCE A WARRIOR
~ NOW AGAIN

The one you look to becomes abusive
The one once worshipped becomes pain
The one you once idolized
Now they treat you with disdain.

We live today and plan tomorrow
We thrive in hope and not sorrow
Eyes are front and that's a fact
Battle makes us tougher
Failure make us strong
Pain is a reminder
Telling us that we belong

The end result inside not grow
The comfort blanket we all need
There for us twenty-four seven
There for everything and not just feed

As you are shifting
Will begin to realize that,
You are not same person
You use to tolerate have now become intolerable

Where you once remained quiet,
You are now speaking
Your truth where you once battled and argued,
you are now choosing to remind silent.

You are beginning to understand
The value of your voice and there are some situations that no
longer deserve your time, energy, and focus as we grow.

Bose Enduwe Adogah

WILL START OVER

(End of year)

End of one is coming
Still almost sane
Will start over
Try again
Has been experience
There's no doubt
Has sometimes made one wonder
Will we see it out

The disasters many through this one
Some are finishing, some just begun
Natural and man-made
Not sure of which am more afraid
For many linked I believe
That, more than anything, makes one grieve
Seen too much suffering, too much pain
Will start over and try again

To be positive, to believe
Some corrections we can achieve
Soon a new data in history
History of mankind – you and me
If join together it could work
If for own comfort none do shirk
Then hopes and chances are a plenty
When we enter Twenty Twenty

In this one each have fought battles
Some won, some lost
Now time for reflection
To count the cost
Then with resolve
Must try again
Will start over
Make things sane

ACHTUNG!! MAYBE

Achtung! Maybe
Know this is crazy
A concept so absurd
Yet the truth has benefits
Surely should be heard

Προσοχή friend! Let's start a trend
One size wears us all
Not the clothes for no-one knows
When from waist can fall

Aandag you who has a clue
Living proof some are
When accept have no regrets
As Nation moves on far

Увага yes – you as well
Look and look again
No discrimination is generation
For world with far less pain

Atención my sun tanned friend
Diverse is so perverse
Unity is family
When shed opinions curse

Zhùyì to my far flung ones
Mediate don't fight
Hostility breeds increasingly
There's no power in just 'might'

Attention please to everyone
Let's stop this while we can
The increase in force as answer
To the questions asked by Man

MY SUBSTANTIVE

It was around at Breakfast time
Again it was at Brunch
It is now at Afternoon Tea
It was when I had lunch

My sustenance is substantive
It comes from, mainly two
They are my food and drink in life
Of whom you have a clue

We are a three course meal you see
Though not as how do think
For each of us plays a role
As another's food and drink

Not physical but emotional
As important true
For like the other energy providers
It feeds just what we do

I guess that one could be classed as my food
One classified as drink
Together pulled back from the abyss
When tottered on the brink

Now they are worth more than Life
More than could ever say
My Wife and Daughter are everything
Throughout my living day

SURFING

One with words and strange ideas
Of love and hate, hopes and fears
Of lots of smiles and equal tears
Gathered over countless years

Sat one Saturday early night
When street lighting glowed so bright
Woke from sleep as thought was caught
Transferred to hobby in which had bought

Tap, tap goes the single finger
As holding Tablet didn't linger
Lest be gone and not shown
The kind of thinking sleep did own

Not distracted by that 'attracted'
Influencing how they acted
Just a simple statement said
From inside a 'resting' head

More in News of dissatisfaction
Seems to be the main attraction
If not abroad then at Home
Guess everywhere including own

A simple thing occurred to one
Imagining if begun
The spectacular of what be
If became reality

Surfing waves of contemplation
What would be like to be one Nation
Oh how could travel oh so far
Hang on a sec! Already are!!

THE PICTURE

I have a picture
On our living room
Wall that reminds me
Of Christmas one of
Life's little treasures
I own

It's a picture of a
Snow scene
That brings back
So many memories
As children make
Their snowman just like
My two brothers and me

With foot prints in the
Snow some big
And some small
And some little
Bird prints right on
Top of the snow

I brought the picture
For the memories
That it holds of all
Those years ago
Back when I was
So young looking back
Now I'm old

Andrew Jones

THIS WONDERFUL WORLD

It's such a wonderful
World we all live in
Just take a moment to look
Around and you'll see
At the scenery all around you now I'm sure
You'll agree

Such beauty we see all around us birds high up
In the trees that sing
Green grass in the spring
And in summer so much
More to be seen

The morning due on the fields and hedgerows
Wild flowers in woodland
And glades were rabbits
And fox Cubs sunbathe
And play

Or the bracing sea air at the
Seaside hills Valleys and
Streams and the snow on
The hilltops in winter
Of this wonderful world
We live in

Andrew Jones

ONCE ~ IT COST

Tobacco smoke drifting slowly upwards
Ice melting in the Glass
Self destruction but not caring
That's now in the past

Nothing much more than just the day
For tomorrow will be the same
So pass it in a semi stupor
Nothing more than name

Old enough to know what doing
Young enough to just not care
Easier to blot all out
Simpler to not dare

Earn enough to keep it growing
Efforts in not showing
At least until days end thrill
Then rubbish bank starts growing

Self destruction an objective
To the tools are so attentive
Ways and means inventive
I became a Master

Once - it cost
Now with what lost
When found a cause to change
Then things changed again

You cruel, cruel thing to now bring
Your cost for what have done
Charged me more than normal
Look at what I have become

MAKING MAYHEM
MUDDLING MINDS

Another block of dysentery
Apart from the Guests involved
To make them semi decent
That problem think I've solved
More firewood if can separate
The others from my bits
The only bit that guarantees
More and more 'like' hits

The left don't know what right is doing
Right just does what pleases
Nothing in this game is 'normal'
Everything me it teases
Making mayhem, muddling minds
What you get is what thou finds
Everything and anything
No guarantees come with these so read them at your peril
Apart from those that please

The talented and then me
The clever then the fool
The need to ride through my diatribe
That, unfortunately, is the rule
The nuggets in the pile of ****
The bits that are so good
Hunt for them amongst my stuff
Need for better understood

Amazed they choose to help me
Grateful that I am
They turn the coals to diamonds
In ways they only can
So I will keep on making mayhem
For know they'll get me through
Muddling minds is where I am
When doing what I do

IN MY HEAD

I came, forgot – forgot a lot
Replacing in my Head
Old no show as new does grow
Peacefulness instead
All that's been just bad dream
All to look forward to now
To get back to those I love
Any means and how

Forgot Hate and to which relate
Found a love instead
That is what now fills me
Fills an empty led
Been and done then carried on
Many are the same
Just another number now
In some departments game

In my head have put to bed
The angst of feeling sorry
This too short for getting caught
With the bit named worry
Bits and bobs not worth the sobs
Just a learning curve
Next time not the same crime
As around situation swerve

Me that be does finally see
The goodness all around
As others say and not for play
Am as sound as pound
So to you look what do
Lead a team of love

THE INK THAT FLOWS

Ever thought that words so caught
About the writer not that written
Ever thought about those fraught
When writing because their mission
Ever knew or had a clue
What experiences they went through
Ever stopped and behind think
As you read and beverage drink

The ink that flows so no-one knows
The pain so buried deep
The masquerade that's writer made
The hurt they silent keep
The more explore to even score
The words that silent spell
In charade for them not hard
To disguise living Hell

The doppelgangers of the spanners
The ones with thoughts do grace
In actions as mere reactions
To fill an empty space
The Creatives amongst natives
The oft chosen but not willing
The ones that care to gift share
Not that of a perfect killing

The ink that flows some hope it sews
That others might be better
With just a verse as is their curse
Paid by letter after letter
Enjoy their labour, even savour
That which they put down
Just remember that in cold December
All need a thick warm gown

BANGERS 'N' MASH

Two fried sausages and some mutilated potato
Smothered in a grave thick
Hopefully with hint of onion
And so dense to mouth will stick

A classic London thing to fill you
As outside the weather's turning
Just the ticket to restore you
As a daily crush are earning

Screw those jellied eels and stuff
Cockles, Winkles and the rest
On a day of cats and dogs are falling
They won't help put hairs on chest

Nah, you need something whole and hearty
That leaves a tummy feeling full
Good old fashioned London stodge
To accomplish is my rule

I WONDER

An anachronism or part of mission
To deliberately mislead
A statement out of context
A false path can it feed

'I'll love you in the morning'
Never mentioned type of love
The one that's purely physical
Or that from the thing above

Relationship or sensationship
A thing to get attention
Superstars who drive flash cars
When 'convenient' love life mention

Sensational or behavioural
Media and hype
We grow and know thought sometimes slow
To recognise the type

I wonder how many true are lost
Because of this common trait
Begin to skim as passing whim
Those of whom just don't relate

It happens to the normal people
It happens to the 'Stars'
Those who use public transport
Those with expensive 'Fars'

Beyond the likes of me you see
So cynical maybe
When life is about attention
Sometimes miss reality

NEVER LET THE

A friend approached one looking glum
For long time they had not seen
Not quite the reception expected
What on earth could mean?
The glum one then did tell them
The glum one spilled the beans
The friend did listen about a life
Then told what it means

Some have been and done
Some never got the chance
Some were born with 'Two left feet'
Still they try to dance
Some get it all, lucky them
Some have to go beyond
Some treat achievement as a given
Some it is so fond

What we get is most we let
Be like me and happier be

So it gives you lemons
Great for that and 'ade'
So it's made you miserable
Well at least something it has made
Never let the downs get me down
Always looked at up
Never gave up on it
Now I sip from loving cup

Like is what you make of it
Wherever it then goes
It is but an entertainer
Creating many shows

CLIMPTIT BIZKIT

Climptit Bizkit went and risked it
Not how did usually behave
Went for broke when thought it joke
Recognition had to save

Climptit thought that it wrong
To be where did not belong
So did try to make a change
From something that found quite strange

Climptit went and stood his ground
Explaining clearly what had found
Other party did not attend
Made it easy to then mend

Climptit spoke as panel listened
From the evidence they did glisten
Something wrong that could make right
Climptit was full of delight

Waiting time less a crime
When known that what to come
Just got caught with the thought
Was not the only one

If their case time did waste
How many others suffer
Spoke to one that had own joke
In waiting room in Wheelchair with a cover

Climptit Bizkit is not finished yet

JUST ANOTHER BIT OF SILLINESS

"Excuse me friend, have you got a light?"
"Yes my friend, I have a torch"
"How in hell is that supposed to light this cigarette?!"
"It will help you find your matches"

When the Grand old Duke marched his men
Up the hill and down again
Did he go to them show
He wasn't some old codger?

Is 'bric a brac' guaranteed intact
Or just some broken mess
Never know so to it don't go
I'm pompous I do confess

If it and that had a spat
Were would writing go?
For if look in many a book
Just not on major show

Twinkle, twinkle little Star
Are you really having laugh
Up close and personal it is huge
Beyond the plot of graph

Nursery rhymes are a crime
As we ourselves get old
Yet they meant so much sent
By adults who were so bold

Cynicism in older prisms
We criticise yet do
Repeat to those growing up
Yes you do too

LOST LECTERN AT EL LIBERATOR

The jungle camp and over ran
Thus the story then began
Of the one who fell out of favour
So the lost lectern at El Liberator
Was not a Church as we regard
More a type of meeting hall
Yet like the person so the place
Into oblivion both did fall

Was not of native common born
More an invader who took by storm
Conquered then converted those
Their opinion it now shows
Into that of disrepair
For when overthrown none did care
To that way to even care
Of something that should not be there

The lectern was discovered
By a team that heard the rumour
Of the Town called El Liberator
Could have been found by some much sooner
The natives all new of the ruins
Had no desire to rebuild
For through tales passed down
Knew that it once did yield

The lectern and the lessons learnt
The outcome when were gone
That who were not invited
Those who could not belong

In the annals of what we did
Somethings perhaps are best well hid

EXPLORING THE ATOLLS
OF AMBITION

So many ventured, so many lost
So many paid the highest cost
So many won, so many gained
So many places with their names

Intrepid folk one and all
Ventured out to answer call
What lies there over yonder
No good sitting here and ponder

Out then into the unknown
For that way the answer shown
Physically and emotionally
A better place we then see

Nothing tried then nothing won
Nothing learnt from different fun
Nothing but the old same, same
No then spreading different name

Exploration of creation
Building of a different Nation
Sometimes sad, sometimes salvation
Repetition through Generation

Use of force not applause
Welcoming much better
No gunshots heard or bomb explosion
Justifies this type of notion

Educated not Dictated
Then a story warm related
In the annals of our History
Far, far better place to be

THEY FOR US

On snow covered Mountains
And muddy field
In air and sea and Terra firma
Those apart would not yield
In day and night
Dark and bright
One thing only
Will still fight

For other people and belief
Willing hardship and the grief
Situations quite unreal
How it was so hard to feel
Yet they stood and stood firm
So rest of world could then learn
That certain things we will not spurn
Freedom's not sold in some Urn

Man and Woman both alike
Took up arms and joined the fight
Not all 'Front line's but suffered same
When war decides to play its game
Is it so wrong to spare some time
To remember them is not crime
You exist because what did
When call went out none then hid

They knew that it would carry risk
The ultimate if be
To leave the land and loved ones
For all eternity
Yet chose they did in deep conviction
Theirs a just and rightfully mission
Many heroes were sadly lost
Other heroes pay the cost

A few minutes of respectful silence
Is that really too much to ask
For those who chose to commit
To what seemed a monumental task

ne obliviscamur

ALGORITHMS

Algorithms are a blessing
Algorithms are a curse
Chopping out the wasted time
Then do something worse
Algorithms don't think!

Black and white - wrong or write
No interpretation
Do what told and tho behold
A confusing situation

The tranquillity of transportation
Being with those with want to be
The second best until can rest
With them in the reality

The grace of face in cyber space
The dulcet tones so clear
The projections without intention
When you know so dear

The abuses from those who chooses
To use for that intention
Not I'm sure that what for
When making this invention

Grown long past and growing fast
The uses it can do
Beyond the scope of which can cope
The 'smart ones' have no clue

Algorithms are a future and a curse

ASKED AN ANSWER
FROM ANONYMOUS

Imagine how to my consternation
The end result of a situation
It was in fact an education
For the purpose of liberation
I asked an answer from anonymous
Thought my query surely obvious
I was merely being curious
Not wasting time what that frivolous

The look, the tone they surely own
For nothing like it previously got
When you think of the depths did sink
That, then somehow, says a lot
Withering and quivering
Under lasers disguised as stare
Message sent that somehow went
"You have the cheek to even dare!"

A purchase lost by head toss
A baffling situation
Almost annoyed by who employed
This bad example of retail station
The shop must like not much selling
When more than me I'm sure are telling
Of being drawn to quiet places
Then find out why when get that face

'A face can launch a thousand Ships'
That one could re-enact Dunkirk
Vitriol purely physical
Why when that feel even go to work?

MY BODY CHOSE ME

Sitting at a beach.
I watch the water ripple
As the waves roll away.

The water, it goes forever.
As far as the eye can see.
Interprets the sense of freedom.
I wish that could be me.

Instead I feel trapped
Inside this mixed up body.
To which I have no way out.

I feed it with Oxygen.
And all good things.
Even give it water
Here and there.
Occasionally making it sing.

Unlike the waves on the ocean
That can be relaxed and calm.
The body, it is twisted.
Each day never the same.
The arms and hands.
They bend and curl.
The legs and feet.
Cramp and twist.
Having no respect for me.

I give my body lots of things
All are good for it, I know.
I feed it with lots of love.
But love it doesn't return.

This body, it chose me.
I never understood why.
I'll continue nurturing
And loving it with
Each breathe I take.
Until the day I die.

For my mind and thoughts
They work just fine.
Dumb I'm certainly not.

Catherine Taylor

EFFORTLESS IS EFFECTIVENESS

Sometimes less is more
Some simple stuff adore
Sometimes but not always
Complicated is but a Maze

Agree somethings are complicated
Until you understand
Yet other things are beautiful
When made by simple hand

The Pyramids of Egypt
Mona Lisa a fine teaser
Stonehenge revenge for what can't comprehend
The Acropolis a crowd pleaser

Simplicity is divinity
In certain situations
Does what does with no fuss
In certain strange occasions

Why bust a gut with tut, tut, tut
When plain simple same will do
Effortless is effectiveness
If one has a clue

Case in point
5 minutes to fill another page

CAN I HAVE CINNAMON ON MY EGG NOG

Can I have Cinnamon on my Egg Nog?
I know that not done thing
Just want to add excitement
Hopefully will bring
Can I be an Australian Santa
In harsh England time of year?
Frost bite to nether regions
Something I don't fear

Can I give Gifts to total strangers
Without worry about the cause
Will I just get a smile upon receiving it
Not some worried pause
Good will and Peace a joy released
Though lost in modern time
Yet being one to promote unity
Surely is no crime

Can I bear a Christmas Carol
Sung just for personal gain
When festivity becomes business
Life becomes a pain
A few months of peace and harmony
Then back to the old same
Diversity and, sometimes, hostility
In our such clever Game

The sellers all do love it
The buyers love it too
Out give the gift of giving
Which then is the fool?
For one night hostilities put aside
At the Christmas Party
Then with added Hangover
Resumed if now less hearty
I guess that I am the pre 3 spirit Scrooge

SOMETHING'S SHRINKING

Something's shrinking and it's not my thinking
It's distant travel that's the past
The world is smaller as we get taller
A history not meant to last

The union is a triumph
If we choose to care
The travel is insignificant
If we choose to dare

Something is shrinking and that's isolation
If that is our choice
Meetings new as wealthy grew
As discovered a new voice

'All for one and one for all'
A famous line that's heard
Spoken in a small situation
Now it seems absurd

Not the line for that still stands
Just the need to have to say
Bygone years with fears and tears
Alas not quite the perfect day

Some still live so cossetted
Some but not a lot
Most are more broadminded now
Appreciation of what got

The easy chance to meet the new
The ease with which can see
The difference in the common
The things that we be

ANOTHER NONSENSE
NOW SHOWS

How many names for how many people
How many different have same name
What do we call a group of gatherings
In this complex convoluted pain
How many strange pronunciations
How to which one call
When have two same, different
Can appear a fool

So Shannon shone a shining light
Dexter delved down deep
Tammy tutted triumphantly
Kelvin a case to keep
Arthur arranged as Arthur does
Fiona forgot that thing fuss
Margaret made and then plans laid
Brian beckoned and Brian bade

My tongue is twisted with head exploding
The more I meet the worse it gets
A rolling 'a' or sharp 't'
Where in it harsh injects
Historical and fictional
All now seem fair game
Only trouble none envisaged
None of us speak quite the same

Trevor tried triumphantly
Echoe lost her sound
Mark is still making one
Patience now profound
Steven/Stephen already a major mess
Catherine/ Caitlin has a difference I confess
Troy for Boy is kind of cool
Hot for girl not so
When computers are choosing disaster names
Our own will surely grow

AN ALMOST SONNET
FOR THE SENSES

The startling glare of the nowhere
The cleansing air so clean
The warming envelope of the atmosphere
Whatever could this mean?
The cutting of fresh water
The wholesomeness of food
The quiet of the present
As opposed from day to day
The mood is quite infectious
Again whatever could this means?

The placidity of relaxation
The comfort of content
The pride of being different
Another day well spent
The gentle closing of the eyes
The gentle sigh emitting
The hope that this is one of many
Outside influence permitting

The subtle note of awareness
The welcome all the more
As recognition is permission
For further to explore
The step back to go far further
The 'timeout' that has things racing
The needed bit for things to fit
To conquer that your facing

The crazy notion that seems a potion
The gift that keeps on giving
The decision done to have some fun
Life is for the living

DISTANCE DOESN'T DAMPEN

An actual in inescapable
A life they did not choose
Yet something out of nothing
When both chose not to lose

One did sit in early hours
What neighbours did call night
Yet to them was different time
So began to write

We are apart but not forever
Soon again will be together
Each have trials and tribulations
Each together in our different nations

The times we spend together
A precursor to some more
A different way experiencing
New avenues explore

Adaptability is vitality
Necessity a must
Driven by the ultimate
In our love we trust

The other read those words said
A tear and smile both came
For as usual thoughts reflected
Passionate yet tame

The wild times were long past
Stability now strong
Mutual support in whatever
Is where they both belong

IF I AM IN A PARADISE

Everything you say to me
Everything you do
If I am in a Paradise
It's all because of you
The moments shared exquisite
The contentment makes me bound
The joy that you have brought to me
The best one I have found

The man who was just getting through
The survivor with no goal
Found the unexpected
That that makes him whole
The thing that he'd been missing
The thing we cannot buy
The reason I do ask myself
The reason and the why

That you chose to bestow your grace on me

Yet complain? Never dear
All I know from day one is that I want you near
Near enough to feel you breathing
Near enough my stress relieving
Near enough to hold you close
Is that demanding? I suppose

I see your face in daytime
I see your face at night
Whenever know that you are there
Everything's all right
Everything you say to me
Everything you do
If I am in a Paradise
It's all because of you

A SINCERE STATEMENT SAID

We go through life making promises
Some we never keep
Various reasons for the failings
Leaving others to simply weep
Then come the ones that mean so much
Move Heavens and Earth to fulfil
Not just because of what was said
It was spoken with a will

A sincere statement said is sacred
To the one who speaks
A sincere statement said is promised
One that vow to keep
No matter what the cost to pay
Regardless of the price
Will achieve despite it all
When find the Rose within the Rice

A sincere statement an undying pledge
A commitment not to break
A set of words that are much more
When that choice do make
Statements said come in many guises
Some are for effect
You only get what you put in
Sometimes even that not set

I vow to keep my promise to get home to those I love
I will move Mountains to keep that promise made
This is not an idle statement
This is not some charade

SAME AGAIN

"Same again?" asked the sandwich
To the Burger by its side
Two days into 'sell by date'
Hardly said with much pride

"Yes, same again" answered Burger
Waiting purchase and then 'nuked'
A new one filling vacancy
When the old one bought then puked

"lucky you" said the Fruit salad
From the shelf above
"At least you get some attention
Bordering on love"

The conversation in the Kwikmart
Between the things that sold
Many are the eye openers
With the things that told

"Anyone got a couch to spare?"
Asked the liquor bottle
"Not me you thing sorry"
Replied the toy car at full throttle

"Just shut up!" said the cup
You all have it good
With me they play
Use then throw away
In some strange Neighbourhood's"

Relation beyond dictation
The secret life of shelf
I have learnt to understand
Now question Mental health

BAD IDEA

Went back to where once did belong
This time though it felt so wrong
Apathy in air strong
This place was not for me
Too much time between us
To many places new
A stranger in my birthplace
Made for a confusing brew

Walking streets that once did walk
No-one knew with whom to talk
Remembering where we scrawled with chalk
If the wall still stood
New street names where once played games
More takeaways than one chip shop
More and different these bus stops
Different the shop names

A Goldfish in a sea of sharks
Just wanting to get out
What happened to my childhood
It leaves it with some doubt
Did I really ever live here
In this strange new place
Was I ever recognised
When someone saw my face

Now have many memories
Few though of this space
Guess that comes with travelling
In lands with different Race
More time spent on foreign shores
As older I do grow
There now more familiar
There now not for show

A LOOK

A look in which I hope you'll find
I am not of some strange alien kind
To one topic will not bind
Even if classes mainly Blind

A look changed in more than one way
Both physical and what may say
Scope in some sense now yesterday
With adaptability I do now play

What's in a look?
Have you heard
That simple line that sounds absurd
Until you realise not all cured
In certain way my thoughts are 'purged'

A look so judgemental
Not the thing that fits
A look that says 'welcome you're
Far more comfortably on this face sits

A look of condemnation
Bitter but better kept
In a place of private choice
When with rage are swept

A look of warmth so welcoming
An invitation to explore
An exchange of who both are
A life lesson to explore

A look took and head shook
When surmise they are a Crook
That accounts they did cook
Until found out when took a look

ASKING ANGELS FOR ADVICE

Angels walk the Earth it's true
I have not one for I have two
When is needed in a trice
I'm asking Angels for advice

Sometimes we needed a different outlook
Are too blinkered so can't see
The wood for trees that envelop
Then come saviours for likes of me

A different slant without a motive
Apart from doing for you best
Words are taken as are spoken
With free will and doubts at rest

Yes Angels come in many forms
With eyes open and are wise
See the one that truly stands there
See beyond the disguise

In truth I have more than two
Others known for what do
Two are 'blood' for they be
Put together – My Family

Others are family too
Some are old and some new
Yet are Angels just the same
Just Angels bearing different name

Benedicite Angeli, qui ambulant in terra

FIXED THE FAULT

In life we face so many challenges
Each from which we do learn
Problems made and some not
Some blindside, some we spot

In a pickle, in a jam
Needed now a Master Plan
No good moping and just coping
Just go forwards – because I can

Took on-board and some stored
If nothing else was never bored
Life's for learning – good and bad
While are learning best times had

Fixed the fault and then forgot
Done a few times, done a lot
Then moved on to pastures new
Found the best thing I could do

Born with space between the two Ears
Some filled up in early years
Still much, much vacuum yet to fill
Slowly filled – filling still

I love the feeling of different trying
Will not run out Time supplying
Avenues and possibilities
To help this one make better me

So come on Fate, play your game
For in strange way are both the same
You play me and I play you
When are curious is what we do

ONCE UPON A TOFFEE TRIFLE

'One up man ship' I despite
As something from them unwise
Room enough for all to be
In a state of equally free
Sooner or later each will fall
Just the timing others call
When enough they have had
Of being put upon and feeling bad

The self imposed Head of Nation
Found themselves in situation
Not the 'love' they did demand
Then it kinda got out of hand
The 'serfs' beneath this 'Rulers' crown
Decided a peg to take them down
Chose a Banquet as best place
To signify their fall from grace

So to be honest I must add
My laughs and cheers I tried to stifle
To see a fools head planted bad
Once upon a Toffee Trifle
To witness it upon the News
As the channels did peruse
Turned factual into comedy
Turned wrong choice into reality

None did stop to give them aid
Around them formed a big Parade
Dancing, singing with such joy
For semi – peaceful did employ

But they surely let their feelings be known

WHO MAKES THE MARKS

History and infamy
Bravery and obscenity
Acts recorded and applauded
Others derided, not much lauded
Some sadistic
Others caring
Both the types
On pages sharing

Who decides and then scribes
What dictates the choices made
Was it the Victims justifying
Was it victims whose clan was dying
Is it through some monument
A work of art to pay their rent
An extinction that we caused
When ancestry, they never paused

I am fascinated by the past
Of that gone and did last
On most types will gaze cast
Sometimes in wonder
Sometimes aghast

Who makes the marks for all to see
Who makes the bits of History
Who does something to be applauded
Something hideous that's recorded
Who and what are these ones that most then know
Who put it out for the big show
Was their actions something pre planned
Did situation just get out of hand?

ANTLERS AT ATTENTION, HORNS A HOPEFUL HARVEST

Men are Stags strutting their stuff
Women a more domestic breed
One meets other and lo and behold
Out pops a new found breed

A mix of both quite unique
Unless, of course, is twins
One or more - who's keeping score?
When Man and Woman wins

Both of the same classification
Just different in a thing called Nation
Both reproduce with same situation
To create new Generation

Man the Stag and Female other
Form a bond we call a Lover
Commit themselves and then cover
Biologically they nearly smother

This is not about the act
This is about a mutual pact
To keep a future preserved, intact
Turning theory into fact

The end result will do again
With another not the same
Another 'mutation' we then name
In the evolution game

Ian Wilcox

CAN YOU CONVINCE

Can you convince that we are Masters
When Corn is burnt but raw inside
Can you convince me that we are Masters
When despite it all can't control the Tide

Can you convince me we are superior
When Nature works in harmony
Can you convince me that we are not interfering
In the way that things should be

We alter for our comforts
We change to make it good
Yet do we really look much further
Is our impact understood

We moan when weather turns against us
We blame everything but our self
For we are focused on one thing
Regardless we seek 'wealth'

Can you convince me that we are not changing
How things are set to be
Can you convince me that our actions
Are not borderline insanity

Easy to gloss over
Moan and groan but carry one
What topic will we moan about
When all the subjects gone?

LET'S AWAKEN THE DOVE

Let's not awaken the Dragon of War
We've been down that route too many times before
All do lose and no-one wins
Innocent pay for our sins

Carnage, destruction long past time
When did commit this heinous crime
Scars are deep in land and living
When its freedom we are giving

Just look back in History
The scars left are plain to see
Bordering on calamity
Imagine how the next would be

Let's instead use our Head
Let down a different path be led
Thought of violence should be shed
Filled with unity best instead

Let's awaken the Dove of Peace
Let's instead that one release
Make this planet a safe place
On which to live with good Grace

Let's unite in one good fight
Let's use our powers for some good
The machines that we have made
Employ, instead, in rebuilding trade

Manpower, resources on which we've spent
Let to where needed then be sent
Some already I do know
Let the others to them go

MY CROWN

My crown I wear as a belt
It keeps my feelings up
My crown I use to hydrate me
It is my coffee cup

And when my crown fell from my head
I could begin to see
That I was not that I was
Was not the true real me
I am not worthy of a crown
For all that I do care
Is the one with which were born
The crown within my hair

My crown I break a piece of it
Each and every day
My crown was made of plastic
So with it do play

My crown it was an ego
That I now do see
My crown was just an open door
Into insanity

And when my crown fell from my head
I could begin to see
That I was not that I was
Was not the true real me
I am not worthy of a crown
For all that I do care
Is the one with which were born
The crown within my hair

SITUATION A CREATION

Ever had that feeling
Life and World against you
Take a moment to yourself
This is nothing compared to true

You are better than have got
You are you - That means a lot
Who really cares about the others
Unless friendship and family covers

First and foremost you are you
You will do what you will do
If they don't know you have no clue
Even knowing, sometimes true

A situation a creation
When do look in retrospect
For without the push it gave you
Never would that dream you get

Negatives and Positives
Are like the proverbial known Olives
Black and Green yet both mean
The image of the Sun is seen

Shed off despair for that's nowhere
You are going places
Be gone forlorn for new is born
With lots of smiling faces

AMIDST CONFUSION CAME CLARITY

The loving couple at awkward stage
Long together now old age
Knew each other better than self
Each one worried about others health

Nag and counter nag did do
If foot fits then wear the shoe
Both were guilty but also Jury
So no words said in tones of fury

As time went on and feelings strong
A climax it did brew
Not quite confrontation just situation
Each aa chance to say what knew

Rather than vocalise
For neither though that would be wise
Decided instead to pen in head
The feelings deep inside

Both did write for other to see
Both four words, not five or three
Both determined and so unity
Amidst confusion came clarity

The couple looked and looked again
Checking writing was not their name
Both were sharing the same pain
When did care but did refrain

Ian Wilcox

AUTUMN FOR THOSE AVARICE

The Spring was fun as begun
To build the nest egg based on wealth
Then not knowing nor were showing
The great impact on their health

Summer came and did gain
In what set out to do
Of the rest? Just second best
For did not have a clue

When can be bought it counts for nought
To appreciate must be earned
Then you know that it can grow
Not just replaced when spurned

With high gain comes a pain
Not now but waiting for
The time to call and watch them fall
As lose what they adore

They've been and done, made a sum
They put enjoyment as a risk
Then do fall as do we all
The Autumn of the avarice

Guess the morale of this verse
Never be that so perverse
To fall into age old curse
Believing everything is money

The best times are when have little
Maybe none, that is true
Then inside you can't hide
Exposed and building a real you

Ian Wilcox

IMAGINE DAYS

The pen did rest from the paper
Another one to be sent
The days of actual efforts made
Tbe effort that was spent
Imagine all the 'Hardship'
That social media blight
The pain of doing something
You actually had to write

Imagine days of bygone age
When to write you had to hold
Not a finger over screen linger
So your thoughts are told
Imagine if not spontaneous
Yet took time to say
Would conversation be so flippant
Would so freely say what say

Was not long ago in case don't know
This was normal thing
Now is part of History
As microchip did bring
The personal stuff of which now huff
That somehow means much more
The knowing in the showing
From a bygone shore

With ink we drink to closer link
A one to one so true
The statement said to the head
You're important you

Ian Wilcox

NOW DUN'S DONE

There was one that wasn't fun
The younger they did mock
Even up to 'social media'
When was seen they did block

Dun decided for a change
Secret lessons did arrange
Then at place not seen before
Dun heard the music so 'hit' dance floor

The moves were of perfection
None were fault with no exception
Flowing smoothly with no pause
A revelation did Dun cause

Now Dun's done the 'Dumb, dumb one'
A different one they be
For up to speed with new creed
They now finally see

The 'Dumb, dumb one' was number one
For a reason that begun
When did stop and just pop
Whatever thought and then run

Just how many honestly know this dance?

Ian Wilcox

SO LOOK

Lodieta tumingin sa mga mata na nagmamahal sayo

The Earth is round and going around
The second part I did
The same things at same time
On emotions put a lid
Not much fun when just the one
In groups consisting pairs
All the awkward introductions
All the half hid stares

So look at how you just now
Fill that empty space
Look at how without a doubt
Put that smile upon this face
So look at what you do mean
To a simple man like me
Look at you and what you do
When said yes to me

Not just in company am complete
Not just more sure when strangers greet
Not just better in company
I am better in just me
I climb instead of staying
I focus – not just playing
I concentrate and relate
I understand true love

I hope you know you helped me grow
Into what stands before
I hope and pray understand when say
It's you that I adore

Ian Wilcox

WE

The traveller landed on barren planet
An empty orb that once held life
The signs were of destruction
The sort that caused by strife
Amongst the ashes found something wrote
Covered by a thick ash coat
What it was, was a final verse
Of a species so perverse

'We came, we conquered, now unheard
We left a legacy that's absurd
We thought it wise to improvise
When, in truth, should have been nice
Not just to each other
That mistake can cover
Yet to that seen all around
That mistake was so profound
We 'ruled' as fools, created tools
To destroy we did employ
Never showing (perhaps not knowing)
The psychopaths enjoy'

The legacy of Humanity
The records found in future
The wounds became so insane
Needed more than suture
Came and conquered, did explore
We built our empires and some more
We sought that thing beyond control
We lived the lie without the soul
Alas too late we now relate
As ashes fall so thick
The sun a distant memory
Radiation makes all sick

Ian Wilcox

SCINTILLATING THE SUCCESS

The true love that's finally found
The no more fishing around
The project finished and applauded
The knowing that it is recorded

The beating illness that before
They didn't understand
So had no cure
That piece of writing in the hand

The growing up despite it all
The raising self despite the fall
Getting up once again
Shrugging off the hurt and pain

The drive towards a known success
The ambition to be your best
The focus on that which right
The willingness to fight that fight

Scintillating is the situation
When one does achieve
Happiness is something blessed
When achieve that you believe

Close to Home or maybe roam
To each a different choice
Just remember that in Life's November
We all speak with memory voice

SOMETIME AFTER SUNSET

The daylight was receding
Sun hidden by the clouds
Made by radiation
Made by those so proud
The red and Black filled the sky
Those still living wondering why
Why and how did come to this
When manmade hell delivered kiss
Now sometime after Sunset
The survivors saw the carnage
Viewed from a remote screen
For still too dangerous to go outside
Unless of suicide were keen

The missiles fell like bad rain
In a worst case ever new Typhoon
Fell across all we call Home
Fell just after noon
Then a single one did speak
Speak for all concerned
They there worries and their woes
Gratitude they earned
Sometime after Sunset
A message clearly heard
Around the world we call Home
'This is just absurd!'

The writer woke from the nightmare
Cold sweat they did feel
For in the back of their mind
Said 'This could be so real'

ALL THE SOUNDS

The walk to Park for a lark
The High street bold adventure took
The casual stroll to feel whole
The cover not the Book
That inside prefers to hide
Ironic at its best
When can't see more words than three
That is also test

All the sounds go round and round
They me nothing much to me
For have got the 'job lot'
From who with meant to be
The noise outside is mere pride
If taken for just granted
When you know it soon goes
If to one are enchanted

Vision was a mission
Part achieved it's true
Yet is more so can endure
After what went through
No sight is blight
Like permanent night
The darkness so depressing
So back some got and means a lot
A sign I am progressing

All the sounds go round and round
Within a single Head
Not that much more need for sure
When found them whom I adore

BLOODSHOT EYES

Bloodshot eyes and not so wise
The pen has gone berserk
When ideas come it is just fun
Writers don't class it as work

Another page to quell the rage
To complete the story see
Be it be fact or, maybe, fiction
Novel or poetry

All Time is right within the plight
No clock to thinking known
Be it dark? That's lightbulbs lark
For making the ink shown

Insomniacs just for cracks
The target almost reached
Another one and nearly done
This driftwood soon be beached

Coffee yes to help the quest
Caffeine is the rule
Alcohol makes flow slow
That's just for the fool

Of clear Mind is productive kind
Just irrational some might find
When takes over in fields of Clover
The hours are no bind

EXCLAMATION

"Hey! Look at you and what propose to do
What,honestly, d you believe?
By doing this and get Reapers kiss
Anything achieve?

Each of us have problems
I'll tell you mine if listen
Then, maybe, some sanity
You might yet achieve

Look at you and what want to do
Make problems for someone else
Just doing job few would do
You're just thinking about yourself

Sod that stare and have a care
Do I deserve to see you die
Do not know but friendships grow
If both of us do try

Come down now you silly cow
You're worth so much better
If no wish to talk we can just walk
Maybe tell me later in a letter

Stop this thing that will misery bring
To more than you do know
Give them a chance when taking stance
To let each one to show

Hard but fair in this cool air
My day has been so stuff
The last thing need for Head to feed
Is some emotional suicide touch"

GOING SLOW WITH
THE FLOW

The story of so many told
The young, the middle and the old
Felt that feeling oh so cold
Turned around and then showed

How many have been there
How many felt but didn't care
How many felt the angry stare
How many just moved on?

Progress made though emotions played
Extreme in Highs and lows
Battle through to achieve new
That's just how this thing was made

The impatience of the youth
Can at times strike as uncouth
Yet the honesty of truth
We've all been and done the same

Reflection of perception
To fix was the intention
Just got caught in light speed brought
Determination in impatient frame

Old comes on and see it's wrong
At least in some of cases
Some need speed - that's agreed
Some are Marathon, some sprint races

Going slow with the flow
Yet is right thing, that I know
Hard for feeling to now show
When all you said was one must go

EXCLAMATION

"Hey! Look at you and what propose to do
What,honestly, d you believe?
By doing this and get Reapers kiss
Anything achieve?

Each of us have problems
I'll tell you mine if listen
Then, maybe, some sanity
You might yet achieve

Look at you and what want to do
Make problems for someone else
Just doing job few would do
You're just thinking about yourself

Sod that stare and have a care
Do I deserve to see you die
Do not know but friendships grow
If both of us do try

Come down now you silly cow
You're worth so much better
If no wish to talk we can just walk
Maybe tell me later in a letter

Stop this thing that will misery bring
To more than you do know
Give them a chance when taking stance
To let each one to show

Hard but fair in this cool air
My day has been so stuff
The last thing need for Head to feed
Is some emotional suicide touch"

FLATULENCE IN AFFLUENCE

Flatulence in affluence
The story of Baked beans
We all know and sometimes shows
Just what that statement means
In and about with roundabout
That we so call digestion
Not for that and that's a fact
Was ever their intention

That devil thing called Broccoli
Has the same effect on me
Rumble thunder from tat down under
In the thing we call Tummy
Noise it grows so everyone knows
You have a slightly embarrassment
Just not of choice this does now voice
An outside message sent

Covers now get lifted
Leg position shifted
Nostrils wake for goodness sake!
As an aroma sifted
Cloying one description
Foul another one
Was plain idiot for what got
When this journey again begun

Anyone got a spare clothes Pog I can have?

HARMONIES A MYSTERY

Paano ko sisimulan na sabihin sa iyo kung gaano kita kamahal?

I came out of curiosity
Found the one that with want to be
Magic stirred and was heard
Results are plain to see

Been the single then senses tingle
A new way was so found
The sensation in acclimatisation
I broadcast and astound

The one begun the 'simple bum'
Grew and so did change
Life it took another look
Gave, until then, so strange

Harmonies a mystery
Yet when find are so worthwhile
Started as a simple word
A brief but magic smile

What more for sure can one explore
Apart from the joy that's found
When find the other half of kind
When meet on common ground

Love you lots my Darling
Love what you gave to me
Love you for still giving
Love with every part of me

ARCHIMEDES SCREW

If Archimedes made a screw
That could do more than things could do
Why then feels so new
When through hard times pull through
Why be embarrassed at what achieved
Why feel humble when some believed
They just knew what have been through
They saw themselves in who call you

Nothing is impossible
Some things may take attention
There are many similar
More unknown so cannot mention
Yet everybody knows somebody
If we but just see
The stranger things arranger
That's a possibility

Not a single person is perfect made
Though some try to say and then parade
Honest truth though sad to say
They are most likely have to be that way
Past goes fast but somethings last
A scar amongst a scarred collection
Some break free by what they be
Some stay trapped in its reflection

If Archimedes made that screw
Then just imagine what you could do
Nothing given on a plate
That's reserved for things like Hate

That's something not worth wasting time on

MEMORIES PARADE
AND NEW LIFE MADE

My past was an experience
One like so many others that go before
My past was just a learning curve
Of feelings – nothing more
What is meant to be was meant to be
Time to just move on
The things strange did thought change
Could almost be a song

Memories parade and new life made
A new way to further reach
Past is vast in hindsight glass
A different way to teach
My old way found a Highway
Not welcome anywhere
For the ones who have begun
To reach out – those who dare

Better am and give a damn
For those who yet to change
Yes I know is hard to go
To life place that's so strange
Yet am proof without aloof
Is possible if you try
All you need is the want to feed
The question that says why

Why try and why put in the time
Why when what am is not a crime?
Why are you not giving self
The benefit of mental health?

You are a survivor so you have skills that others need

PARISIAN PATHS (AND AUTOGRAPHS)

We met in London and had plans
We would together see the world
That was wishful thinking
Now it seems absurd
Time is judge and judge did do
I was not the one for you
So travel plans are now on hold
Until destiny is to me told

We made movements under moonlight
Danced deliriously under Sun
We set ourselves a promise
That came so much undone
It was not meant to be
In harsh reality
I just was not the one

Parisian paths and autographs
The dreams we don't complete
The want to go but get no show
Not like when first did meet
Melancholy made a moment
That moment went too fast
The image was immaculate
The image didn't last

We walk away and both do pray
The other one will be okay
Yet the feelings are still reeling
What more can we say?
The been and gone of forlorn
The chasms it does leave
The quiet time that both called mine
That love chose to deceive

SORRY MATE

It was the early hours
There or Four – I'm not sure
When met the one who 'found 'a cure'

A vertical phenomenon
The type that is so common
Then began the 'Master plan'
Don't upset but go
The sway betrayed and so laid
The mission decision got
Truth be told might soon have hold
Of an inebriated sot

Who are you and what you do
For just met so have no clue
Let's just make this painless

Sorry Mate but can't relate
You're breathing what did drink
It's flavour I can't savour
Have trouble just to think
You amaze in your stupor haze
How you even stand
I agree, though not financially,
A good night out is grand

What's that you said? You're off your head
Best place for you is in your bed
Best of luck when you wake up

The joys of the affluent young
Before responsibility has begun
Then both time and pocket change
Are of the past and something strange

Ian Wilcox

A SWAM SWUM

Sometime in a summertime
A Swan swam royally
It was seen and knew what mean
As it swam just past me
Sometimes in a Summer time
Seems a distant memory
When days are cold and shorts on hold
Goosebumps not want to see

Sometimes in a lifetime
We make choices for the best
Sometimes they turn out wrong
With hassle and the rest
Sometimes all seems sunshine
Sometimes all seems snow
That's just a perception
The way that things do go

A swan swum passed me gracefully
Had realised and didn't care
It had been living long enough
To now just no longer care
What comes its way it will stay
It belongs and it does know
That's what makes it so majestic
It has learnt to grow

CALLED AND COLLECTED

Called and collected
A mother way was taught
Been and came now in same frame
In situation not fraught

The mystery of complexity
Suddenly seems clear
The value shown of them known
The far and those dear

Called and was answered
No message service shown
The answers are the simple not disasters
When they become your own

Not what meant was that sent
Still I had to pay
Hey Ho Hey Ho and on we go
Tomorrow's another Day

Called and got a shock
The delivery a surprise
Guess in hindsight it was not right
With experience becoming wise

Everything for a reason
Reason for everything
Just wish was more selective
When some shock does bring

CONTENTMENT, RESENTMENT AND SETTLEMENT

The contentment found at start
The filling of that part
The warm glow when think you know
You've finally swapped love Heart

The beauty of falling in love

You cold hearted thing to this bring!
Shattered and dejected
I gave to you all I could do
You sent it back 'Rejected'

The anger of a failed romance

Ok let's explore what now more
Friends or drift apart
Let's move on from that that's gone
Make a fresh new start

The settlement

The things I've been and places been
Another living life
The ups and downs - smiles and frowns
Then I met my Wife

Wife a term but nothing more
For better half you see
Filled that missing with her kissing
That is purely ecstasy

EVERYTHING AND ANYTHING LEAD TO A SOMETHING OR A NOTHING

The one chose to mix with 'meek'
Those who glory didn't seek
Those with manners and some style
Those who don't love to revile
Unfortunately along did meet
Those who with this so not greet
Just moved on to that new
For were confident so could do

"How many steps must one take
To a journey that they make
How many are the footfalls
Before considering themselves as fools
How many times inflict the crime
Of judging others before them self
How many know that ignorance shows
When obsession becomes wealth"

So one wrote
Asked one out of curiosity
Is this their nature to be offensive
Is it just some jealousy?
Self opinionated as when stated
An irritation – nothing more
Each can choose their own views
Blatant insults I abhor

They think they're clever and with wit
Yet come across as some strange twit
They like to see their own name
In another's shared thoughts frame

FEELINGS OF FORGOTTEN FELLOWS

The day is young and just begun
The hour quite and 'tame'
The thoughts drift back to certain acts
Of many cannot now name

The bits of past that weren't meant to last
Yet somehow still remember
This time be in January
Not like last in cold December

Strange how when am relaxed
The 'logic library' starts to act
The bits that are buried deep
Yet has decided wants to keep

The friendships made that didn't meet the grade
For reasons to many to say
Some where things just drifted apart
Some who can now not see another day

Then comes the ones before my time
Those that gave me what and when
The chance you see to be free
To think and write with pen

Feelings of forgotten fellows
Known and those unknown
That gave their all so I can call
The next experience 'own'

FLIPPANT IN THE FRIVOLOUS

'The thick skin had a whim
To say what needs said
Before explore something more
Totally leaves in bed

A laugh, a joke, a reason for a laugh
When one know and then shows
Don't seek request for autograph

A decision to take derision
As part of what you do
Insults are expected
Just give me something new

Been and done and carried gun
Words are not that hurtful
When seen what small metal does
The reality is truthful'

Said one who become
Different from their past
Hate is state so mitigate
For Hate just cannot last

BOUGHT MY TICKET

I've bought my ticket to afterlife
Found and married so now have Wife
Between us we have made a gift
Every day my spirits lift

She will carry on the legacy
That some are foolish and call me
Been just doing what all do
In that respect nothing new

Done nothing special - apart
From a certain two who own my heart
Done nothing - can't even sing!
Thank goodness that not passed on

Bought and paid by what helped made
To be honest I didn't do much
The Apple of my eye did most
The way it works and such

Yeah I bought my ticket
Reservation yet confirmed
Not ready for a legacy
No wish for ashes nor inturned

Just bought my ticket and nothing more

COME YOU BEAST

The one stood at the fork in road
A decision, now was made
For was not fork in the physical
Was not open to that 'Trade'

It was a thing inside them self
It was a matter of Mental health
It was a choice to move on
A decision to carry on

They wrote a note to pin to wall
A statement said and seen by all
They might have stumbled but didn't fall
To that rejected they did call

"Come you Beast – try to feast!
You'll find me hard to chew
I am not morsel that you expected
I am something new!"

They chose to be the true person they are

BLUE
THE EVER AFTER
BLISS FULLNESS
IN BLUE

CHERISHED MEMORIES

Memories that
Last a lifetime
In our hearts
And minds each day
Moments that we cherish
No one can take away

Memories of friends
And loved ones
Events that happened
In the past times that
We'd forgotten seems
To come back in a flash

All those family times
Spent together, now
So very long ago
As we grow old together
In the house that
We called home

All those happy memories
That just last a whole lifetime of so many Christmases together so
Many good and
Happy times

Andrew Jones

EVERYTHING FOR REASON

Got limited sight but that's alright
Gave a chance to see
The other side that most try to hide
Yet is in fact a reality
Got to go to that not show
To those unlike their own
The world unheard by fit unserved
By Life in all it's commutations

Been one of those as past shows
Not now I do say
Changes made when things played
And boy! They can some cards then lay
After shock just took stock
Adapt then overcome
Funny though when it did show
Not the only one

Sad, forlorn has been and gone
So has the half empty Glass
Half full now and somehow
This attitude will last
What's meant to be was meant to be
Pointless living in the past
Life is one mother Rollercoaster
This one goes too fast

P.O.E.T.

There comes a time when things begin
There is a stirring deep within
The need to do something more
The wish to visit foreign shore

Literally or physically
Just the something need to be
The excellence of humanity
Is when, with limits, we can be free

The chance to dance with circumstance
The freedom to just feel
The excitement of the previous extreme
The knowing that you are real

Boy to lad and then to Dad
A journey am still on
Yet with every step stronger get
When realise that I belong

Belong to something bigger
This misfit, sometimes sinner
Realise I was beginner
In something I could be winner

Not of everything just myself
When adapted to different health
The old me went on the shelf
A memory and nothing more

Proud Of Everything Tried
To say not would have lied
Though have no sense of pride
Just satisfaction deep inside

Are you Proud Of Everything Tried
In life and in whatever do
For truth be told if I may be so bold
They are all the making of you

Everything accomplished
Every mistake that each have made
Joined into the person now
So to each a Thanks was bade

Promise Only Evolves True
With each thing we try to do
Some repetition for perfection
Some for have no clue

A whim or flight of fancy
Curiosity or dare
We enter into that unknown
Then results we share

I am a breathing P.O.E.T.
At least I try to be
My life is fuller than could be
Just this side of sanity

ICE CREAM'S NICE CREAM

That bitter battle, war of words
The chunks fly off even if absurd
Vitriol like Richard third
Should be kept inside never to be heard
Annoying age of aggravation
Made to last a thing of past
Failure now built in
Things that bought or in life taught
Discard to then begin

You've been, I've been
All done and all seen
Nothing matters if a dream
In the end Ice cream's nice cream
Maybe wet and maybe cold
Something though – never old
Disappears with heat of tears
Then go out for another sold

The maze to faze the inner gaze
The wall that is not there-
The barriers that are hate carriers
The blocks when do not dare
The easy option that is no option
The quitting before starting
The quick release that another please
Two Solicitors in fact
Add cost to lost as salt frost
When neither had much tact

You've been there as I've been there
Though just not that far
Sometimes true, best thing to do
Just not some old car
Don't love waste to just replace
By some new and shiny version
Love means love and not some glove
Not some cruel perversion

TWENTY ~ TWENTY
VISION MISSION

The end does close on another chapter
Mixed bag it had, you'll agree
Some of it were works of wonder
Some were plain insanity
Done and now can't be repaired
Done and from it can we learn
To correct the mistakes made
To expose the big charade

We're getting better, slow but sure
Yet are long way from the cure
Money made in violence
Doesn't help with recompense
Eyes are glued to a screen
Not around and what does mean
Let's lift our heads and take it in
Then together we can begin

A new Decade, a new Year
Let's start by stopping all the fear
An end to all the contradiction
Harmony
Our Twenty - Twenty Vision mission
Not in visual for too hard
When biology plays the Joker card
Yet in something can attain
When from biased we refrain

So Happy New Year one and all
Wherever, whenever it will fall
Time zones separate, that is true
Yet still we talk me and you
If we can nowadays distance converse
Surely we can beat the curse

WHAT TO DO WITH THOUGHT NEW

The ink drips on the paper
Hesitation in the act
Is this really worth the showing
No question but mere fact

Comfort in the holding
Irritation of no use
The words don't flow as what you know
Conscience of abuse

The heady days are over
Never started if am true
Yes my name is now out there
Yet am still the same as you

Explosions and then barren
Switch to different for a change
Back to that I know

So what to do with thought new
Write or put on hold
Never knowing when right time showing
Be subtle or be bold?

I guess that we will both have to see

PRECIOUS GIRL.
OUR MIRACLE

When I met your Dad.
He told me a story.
It goes something like this.

As a young lad
I went to school.
And did the things
I had to do.
As well as being a Brother,
To 2 Sisters.
I was also the only Son.

Been blamed for everything
I got to understand ways of life.
And how different things,
In life are really meant to be.

At the age of 17.
I did leave the Family home.
I went to join the army.
After serving my country,
I left and got a job.
Going from one job
Straight into another.
I did a bit of this and that.
Constantly learning more.
I became quite the all-rounder.

My life, it was all mine.
Though never felt complete.
Something within was missing.
I had no idea what it was.

Years had gone by.
I took a little holiday
To the Philippines.
It was to be the
Holiday of s lifetime.
That it certainly was.

It was there I met your mother.
Beautiful and loving she was.
Each time we met up
We became much closer.
Falling deeply in love with the other.
It was time I marry her.
Showing the world she was mine.

We decided we'd start a family.
Then soon after that,
We created you.
The very thing to making my life.
100% totally complete.

It was 20 years ago
You came and joined us
No 2 prouder parents
Would you ever find.

Your mum with all
The motherly instincts.
Me, a blubbering mess.

You our precious Daughter?
Stole the floor.
Then took the lead.
You showed us was life really about.
With little smiles and laughter.
Tears and crying too.
Teaching us as went
You our precious Daughter
Taught us more about living
Then life did itself

Watching you grow
Through different stages.
School. Teenage hood.
Then into quite a young lady.
Over time you discovered
What you were to be.
Doing a course in Criminology.
You decided would be best

You put your head down
Studying your very best.
You would call in times of help.
Making me so proud.
Now the time for study
Has come to the end.
Time to put what you learned
Into real life reality.
Turning the wrongs to right.

Today is your Graduation day.
A day you truly deserve.
Receiving certificates that say
Congratulations to MJ.
Job very well done

Unfortunately due to circumstances
To of no fault of our own.
I Can't physically be there.
But with my heart and soul.
And my thoughts and spirit.
Right there beside your lovely mother.
In the very front row.
Us. The luckiest parents ever.
With all the love in the world
We proudly look at you and listen on.

Thank you my dearest Daughter
The miracle of my life
You changed your mum's and my life
To something I can't explain.
You and mum. My very Angels.
I love you both unconditionally.
This you must never doubt.

Catherine Taylor

H.B. PENNY

A name became a friend
The modern internet trend
Though one became much more
As a relationship did explore

Half the world it hails
The penner of the tales
Others will catch up
As read while drink they sup

The Lady of so many virtues
In what do and is
The meeting with the Wobbly
Is unadulterated pure bliss

Today's your day so may I say
H.B. and fond Thank you
For giving us without a fuss
The warmth that you do

An H and B to you from me
Amongst the loving crowd
I just put in Ink dear friend
For voice is not that loud

Wishing you many happy returns of the day
May your next year be as exciting as the final days of this one

Hehehe
Okay it is a pencil grade and not a pen but it is also
Happy Birthday my awesome dear and valued friend

SPARE A THOUGHT

(A poem for every Christmas)

That time draws near for festive cheer
For some but not for all
The old and young that have forgotten fun
Because of loneliness or fear
When others answer the 'evil' call

Near and far everywhere are
It will not discriminate
The 'good' is purely misunderstood
When is 'right' to simply Hate
When you are smiling others are dying
Through no fault of own
Some for real and some with feel
Though not all is shown

As that time draws near with those help dear
Not all are likewise blessed
The ones not seen but doesn't mean
We can simply rest
Spare a thought for those with nought
Whilst we with riches overflow
The ones that have just their skins
Most often it's on show

The season not for all beliefs
That I understand
Yet surely the attitude of help
Is one in which all can lend a hand
Humanity and poverty
Go much higher than what we think
Starvation and thirst the real curse
As others eat and drink

Merry Christmas if you are fortunate enough to enjoy it

THE CARNIVAL WHEN
NO WHEREWITHAL

The hurried checking of the pockets
The frantic scenes that play
The seller standing patiently
The look on face to say

The silence speaks as embarrassment leaks
The realisation hitting hard
The items there before you
Yet you've forgotten card

The unheard tapping of impatient foot
Unheard but know it's there
The fifteenth check of pockets
Look up if you dare

The sudden worry of a queue
Gathering behind
As frantically and Illogically
A means to pay you find

That sudden downfall of embarrassment
The look up with the guilt
The honesty when plain to see
You've left it on the quilt

"Can you put them to one side please?
I will be back for them in just a moment"

NEW BUDS

Winter Solstice has come, been and gone
Time for fresh beginning
Slowly turn the change of life
That has most things start 'singing'

Animal, Plant, Reptile too
Enjoy a bit of Sun
Slowly presence starts to show
A new year begun

New attitudes and perceptions?
New outlook, perhaps reflections?
Lots of promises for good intentions
Many though mere misconceptions

New Buds born in coming months
Adaptions and additions
Some may fall along their paths
Others though achieve fruition

Physical and non physical
All do count the same
Some seem almost instantaneously
Others need long Time frame

The important thing is progress
In whatever shape or form
The much needed exploration
Of that when it was born

Odd hours living
A spear of light bursts through gap in curtains
Giving me the hunch
To my surprise it's now sunrise
Almost time for lunch
Breakfast as the date does change
The weirdness all is giving
When one does choose to 'normal' lose
Engage in odd hours living

Ignoring that which body knows
Disregarding what eyes show
Instead, are 'being' where wish to go
Perking up when should be low
Around 'mid afternoon' comes reality
With things to do and people see
For they exist in what is known
As a real current now Time Zone

Real for them though not for you
So are restricted at what can do
In my world not understood
Why in 'my morning' vacuuming's not good
I am up when them in bed
Why not consider me instead
I try to sleep as you enjoy
A good night out or latest 'toy'

At weekends staggering Home at brunch
A 'good night out' was had I think
More decoration on the pavements
As rid yourselves of food and drink
The conversations between nations
Pass my time so quick
I enjoy the bold and coy
While you are busy being sick

YUK~A~DUCK

I dodged left when should have right
There began my woeful plight
On my face, under hat
Hit the snowballs with a splat
More than just water got
Was it blood? Nope, just snot
To go with two eyes don't see
A constant stream of profanities

For was just walking to the shop
When said object did I cop
Assailant quite unknown to me
Cue more directed obscenity
How they laughed at what had caught
For no manners surely taught
A clip round ear a sudden urge
Yet would result in Court case surge

A shake of fist must suffice
To convey this was not nice
Followed by an old school trick
Made a snowball containing brick
Luckily my aims not good
For might have killed I understood
Scared them though and they did scatter
When windscreen on parked car it did shatter

Then some bloke had the nerve
To say my fault for I did swerve
So made another and aimed right
Bang on target!! Double sight
Wrong I know but felt good
Helped relieve the stress
Of looking like some drowned rat
When another in similar mess

BAMBOOZLING BUS RIDE

"So you don't go where sign does show
Together with the App
You have never heard of stop
That where your number's sat

You must stop at it at least twice each shift
Yet say is not on route
Which part of simple question asked
Is bit that can't compute
How about this one or maybe this one?
Ahhhh that helps the riddle
For you see, between you and me
It's in the bloody middle!"

Bamboozling was the Bus ride
By driver with no clue
Of the route that they drove
Connecting One and Two

Are we even on right way to go?
I just simply have to trust
That sometime before New year
Will reach the place I must

Can't enjoy the ride of new ride
When driver I can't trust
Just sit here with sense of fear
That know where go I must

Checking every Bus stop
Compare to printed sheet
Am I any nearer
To getting off this seat?

Ian Wilcox

IN ECHELONS OF
DAYS BYGONE

The 'superior' are inferior
Rule by intimidation
Deception by reflection - the modern world invention
How to 'rule' a Nation
Time goes fast back into our past
The old way but disguised
We procrastinate yet can't relate
The impact made upon our fate
Hopefully will, sometime still
Before it's all too late

So much war becomes a bore
When we inflict on foreign shore
We all deserve so much more
When in harmony can explore
Alas no time soon
The modern trends call the tune
Violence in video gaming
All shoot to kill or sometimes maiming
Our impulses need some taming
Before we become a better thing

Now I sound like some lame Preacher
Maybe some forgotten Teacher
Yet I am a forward reacher
To that in which I believe
We have the chance before last stance
We have a choice to make
Do we destruct because F'ed up
Or do we cycle break?
That's a question for another day but the seed has been sown

KARMA CAME A CALLING

Another day - another play
Without the one called Wife
Another year, another tear
In this game called Strife

New decade for new things made
No looking back just yet
On we go, to what don't know
Just the pace I set

Another goal to get things whole
Unity my mission
To see for real has much appeal
For this one of restricted vision

Then I woke up to who I am

The 'perfect' day was dawning
Prospects for the morning
Gone the time for yawning
Karma came a calling

Not much change but a date
New numbers now I can relate
I alone hold future fate
I am one much determined

Another step to where will get
A simple change in ink
New number now to put on forms
It changed within a blink

Twenty Twenty I do laugh

THE PRE 7AM IMPROMPTU COLLABORATION

Situation Normal
Another day, another Dollar
So they used to say
Somehow true in what we do
Then comes time to play
Play we do though with no clue
Where this thing will lead
Just satisfaction in interaction
As pleasure choose to feed

Just another day
And another dollar
Some street sellers
Shout out while
Others just holler
And it all depends
On the life we lead
If we cut ourselves
Do we just bleed

Just another day so come what may
Nothing too much trouble
Getting by with reason why
Make Castles from our Molehills
You and I and many more
By just simply doing what we do
Show the world that be that we can see
Each waking is something new

For together we both walk
That thin poetry line
All the way through
Space and time
And putting words
Together and some
That rhyme

Poetry for you and me
For others different things
Each have goals to satisfy souls
Achievement in what brings
The important thing is a small one
Yet larger than itself
The quest to go one more step to know
The drive to Mental health

It's just larger than life
Sometimes trouble
And strife but we will
Them win through coz its
what writers do
Never surrender nor
Let the win as I say
Sat in the chair with
A little grin

So we say come what may
No one thing'll get us down
Maybe the odd slight disappointment
Merely produces frown

So just think what
You may in this mad
World of today where
All things are different
Each minute of the day
For just whatever we do
Or whatever we say

Life is of living each
And every day

Andrew Jones and Ian Wilcox

MADE THE MAN

The past was rocky that I grant
Of some experience with a chant
The past before that I don't talk
It just taught me to walk the walk
The behind me is behind
More adventures in the future find
Not those of the single soul
For now have family that makes me whole

The path has been rocky true
As progression nothing new
Just being me and do what do
Believing someday will come through
Nothing's ever boring
When do look ahead
Stagnant is a common curse
I choose advanced instead

The pitfalls are original
Another learning curve
Yet as part of real me
Problems I won't swerve
Many different forms they come in
Many ways I beat
For I am now in better place
In truth it is so neat

I am quite sure
I know I can
For making memories
Made the Man
Not much I'll grant you. Understood
Yet I am me
With Parenthood

CHRISTMAS SEEMS SO WRONG

Christmas lights don't seem right
Too bright and far too strong
Christmas songs are plain wrong
When are not where you belong

Christmas joy hard to employ
When you are alone
To Christmas cheer one gives a sneer
When are not at Home

Those lucky ones that are having fun
Those who to which it all seems right
Lucky you, I just get through
Wanting Christmas night

Then is over for another year
Maybe different come next one
Then, maybe too, can see it through
With company not just one

Alone at Christmas I now know
Through circumstance not choice
This insight I now write
To give to others voice

Those untold, Homeless and old
Many more reasons why
That when you cheer with food and Beer
They go hungry, cold and cry

Christmas seems so wrong when feel don't belong
For many we this day forget
Take some time to correct this crime
A new feeling let us set

MYSTICAL EXPLORATION

Who is me and what am I?
Do we bother? Do we try?
I am me and do what do
Not the same but how are you

Nothing much but is such
Until the person in someway touch
Be it good or be it bad
An experience never had

A chance encounter or arranged
Still not ready for that changed
A new perspective, new outlook
If nothing else then that took

Deeper into oneself go
The more you meet and then know
The greater you, you can show
As adapted, as do grow

Wow!! Deep!!

I like to play with the Squirrels
I try to chase with no success
Those critters run up things impossible
Need Crampons and nothing less

I sometimes mull over choice of clothing
Not what needed but its colour
Does this one go with that one
Should I change this or change the other

What was that noise from next door
That strange knock just past four
In the morning not afternoon
Was noticeably for way too soon

Oh Two Thirty and am hungry
What time is right for ones Breakfast
Then the question of cold or cooked one
How my stomach shall I test?

Another glimpse into the mystery
The mystery of me
The simple answer is there before you
You simply get what you do see

WINKLES TICKLE

Seafood is an abomination
Forget the day or the occasion
Jellied Eels are just a quirk
Pot of stuff drives me berserk
Shrimp a pickle
Winkles tickle
Cod a sickle
Prawns in middle

Out of salty water
That itself is clue
When have to thoroughly wash it
Is it good for you
Need to add a dressing
For it good to eat
It bloody swims in water
Not walking on their feet!

If were Shark for a lark
Maybe try but not
Am a bipod on dry land
So that menu is forgot
If hoof or paws I'll maybe pause
Not a thing that swims
If has a tail for it to sail
Not my kind of whim

Give me red or don't relate
Okay, maybe, white on plate
Nothing wrong when on land strong
That in water body hate
Leaves and trees hunger relieves
Yet want more than Cow food I'm saying
Just not that that lives in water
Is all that I am saying

I BLEED

The one put down the paper stack
That had to read before completing
The pain to gain,hopefully, again
The opportunity of meeting
That autocrat that was at
A meeting once before
Who in derision made decision
Before walking through the door

I bleed and need help to feed
Is that so hard to comply?
If it is then what's the twist
When not checking reason why
Number recitals are not problem
If did look would see
Better than I can now
Registered am me

Not that this concerns you
For I have a hunch
Get through me quite quickly
Then can go to lunch
Another name in same game
To you am nothing more
Another face to fill some space
I must be such a bore

Sorry I delayed you
From something so much better
Like checking on your Instagram
Or composing personal letter
I am a pain from which gain
A monthly salary
Yet I am not worth a look
At whatever I might be

PHANTOMS FLY OVER FORMER FIELDS

On a porch seat by a door
Eyes gazed surroundings, did adore
A new beginning – back to start
Conscience clear and strong of Heart
A victim once but now no longer
Did not cower – became stronger
Man nor beast will intimidate
When cause right and will great

The Lady had been through much in life
Been a lover, mother, Wife
Seen the highs but also lows
Been to places no-one knows
Yet still standing, tall and strong
'I am here and I belong'
Lost some skirmishes but won her war
Became the one she was before

Now the pleasantries did see
Injustice placed in History
Never again second class be
When determined equality
Right from birth and nothing more
Right not dependant upon which shore
Right as equal – nothing less
Right is right- let's pass this test

Physically man is stronger
Though not always or much longer
Different strengths come to the fore
When go through childbirth with whom adored
Partnerships are Mix'n'match
Are whatever way you hatch
No simple rule to all cover
When is Teammate, also lover

SANGUINE IN THE SEASON

Another tick on a list
More to just forget
Another hurdle hurdled
Now again am set
Another accomplishment accomplished
Forward now can look
Experience not wanted
When 'mistake' I took

So one step, getting closer
To where my heart must go
One bit of the nearer
To the love I know
One task of the many
That their love does drive on
One piece of the puzzle
To place that I belong

A journey that is different
From that I had planned
The original that was made
When asked you for your hands
A cacophony of confusion
A strain for all involved
The picking up of pieces
As the challenge solved

Each day getting nearer
To where want to be
A Christmas with my loved ones
Together you and me
Until then just have to mend
That inside and that out
I am not giving up
Of that have no doubt

SHOULD I CHANGE THINGS?

Thinking of my life,
And all the things I've been through.
Would I go back and change things?
Maybe I would.
Or perhaps maybe not

Being tight, on edge,
Body out of control.
Medication given to help
Take control of this twisted body.

I learned to cope.
Do things for myself,
In a weird and strange way.
Thinking back
I wouldn't change that.

School was good.
I learnt a lot.
We all look different
To the outside world.
They were hard but good years
My body was getting stronger.
The more I did,
The better I got.

Later I fell in love.
And had a child of my own
Always thinking,
Will he be normal?

Or maybe like me.
Normal he was.
No. I wouldn't change that either.

I have lived through many things.
Each of them helping to be strong.
Some things would make me question,
Why did happen to me?
I think we all think that.

Now things in my life
Seem to be slowing down.
And thinking back,
All the times I've screamed
Why me? What did I do so wrong?

Would I turn back time,
And change things here and there?
Not a chance.
For all things that have happened,
Whether good or bad,
Have shaped me to who I am today.
With family and friends.
Enemies as well.
I've even found my very best friend
In a way, my soul mate.
Would I change that?
Never in a million years.

Catherine Taylor

FIGHT YOU OR IGNORE YOU

Simply
Taking
Relentlessly
Ever
Staying
Subtly

You are a menace, an abomination
You cover all, each generation
You change the ones personality
You deprive them of what could be

Somewhat
Troubled
Reaching
End
Silent
Stalker

Why do you exist in ones life
Me, my Daughter and my Wife
You cut deeper than the Knife
Giving nothing more than strife

Sensitive
Times
Relating
Everything
Somehow
Stupid

Be gone you vile vermin
Not sure why did begin
Nothing but personal sin
I will not let you win

SHADOW TALK

When walk the walk

The one that stands for righteousness
Yet can be your ultimate pain
The one that has a lot to lose
Yet nothing much to gain
The one that has been sent by others
Too scared so they do hide
Behind some desk in distant office
Soothing their self pride

The one that does 'the hard yards'
So others can then rest
The one that has decided
To face that hardest test
The one that is committed
Come the rain or sun
To see this through until some end
To do what they must do

The one that sacrifices pleasure
Yet tries to hide the pain
The one that pays the highest price
With so little gain
The one seen on News
When something 'right or wrong'
The one who comes back just to find
They truly don't belong

Yes Shadows talk when walk the walk
More than most do know
The longer that each day becomes
The longer that they grow
The ones who made the choice and paid
Not the ultimate but close
The ones who after said and done
Their own cost never shows

FAR FROM HOME AND FEELING WORTHLESS

(Typhoon Phanfone and the Philippines)

Those I love are suffering
Mother Nature's curse
Far from them is killing me
She is doing worse

The time to try to put aside
The time my feelings hide
The time that I should be there
The chance to if not cure then share

The News shows what are going through
Nothing new to them it's true
The extent of what can do
When Mother Earth makes strange brew

Destruction on a grand scale
Can but sit, look on
As the land I now call Home
Takes a beating, a beating strong

Consolation if right word
Somehow saying seems absurd
Knowing that my family's safe
When in the midst of this wraith

Far from Home and feeling worthless
The lowest emotion one can feel
Never really understood
Until the time you feel for real

Sorry Family for not being with you
Sorry for not this thing sharing
Please understand is not my choice
Please don't think that I'm uncaring

SHIP IN BOTTLE

Heating on by tapping screen
Not even being Home
Access to our personal lives
By those who are not known
Food delivery by computer
Items we don't see
Consumables with short shelf life
Not really is it me

Dating by a screen shot
Lottery if you please
Some are genuine that is true
Some just like to tease
Lessons solved by Google
If know what to type
Along with the sensational
Alone with all the hype

Ship it sits in Bottle
Internet, it sits in car
We have progressed in leisure
Ask oneself how far?
Fingers must be getting bigger
One or two at least
All the work their having
Muscles they do feast

Look at what you're reading
Look on what it is
If not ink and paper
Then you get the gist
Tech dependant we've become
Lost those simple things
They joys of actual doing
That satisfaction that it brings

ANACHRONISMS IN A MIGHTY COLUMNS

We all judge and we all hide
Though work and pleasure go side by side
Paid to do what's best for all
Then the money starts to call

Conflicts of conscience, some might say
Which one will be the best pay?
Some take money over good
That, to me, so not understood

Just a number - not a name
Just a piece of work to do
Prejudiced by the mood that current
Not by simple you are you

Wake up, get up, go to work
Hope to climb advancement steeple
Yet the work is not just 'case load'
When your job means other people

Callous creatures sub contract
Have no care - that's a fact
Hated equally by the others
Victims and those who Department covers

Sleep well you piranhas
Sleep well knowing that you lost
Sleep well in your little bubble
Never caring what the cost

CRACKERS IN 'THE KNACKERS YARD'

Orville joked with Stanley
Susan joined in too
Petula would have done so
But had to go to the loo
The old ones are the best ones
Many they do say
Brightening up with a laugh
An otherwise dreary day

Maud applauds as William 'Lords'
Staff just have a laugh
Celestine pretends she's Queen
Ask if any want autograph
Old 'blind' John giggled strong
Together with 'mad' Mazie
Them in charge found it hard
To not call them all as crazy

Bill and Ben the once Mail men
Cavorted with abandon
Trish and Shirl did a twirl
That made the male heart gladden
Fun was had in place sad
Because of what it was
The place you see that could strip dignity
If it ever had

So crackers in 'The Knackers Yard'
Fun, frivolities
Never is one just too old
For hilarity
Attendance and attended
All having a good time
Passed the day in much same way
Morning, Noon, sleep rhyme

ONE WANDERED AND ONE WONDERED

If this world was small and knurled
Would something take it and it hurled
For as is is not much good
When examined, understood

If this Globe were a Robe
Would other life forms care to probe?
Examine with the thought to buy
Would they be interested and why?

If Human race lived up in Space
Would it learn to have more grace
For it lacks, and that's a fact
The simple skill to interact

If body change was less strange
Could we simply just arrange
The meeting mutual of other covers
As just friend if not lovers?

So many questions need solution
As we kill with our pollution
Add manifestation to the equation
Are we not just one salvation

We write and read but don't read what's written
For with technology we are bitten
Tap of screen doesn't mean
That from experience knowledge glean

One wanders and one wonders
Is that person you
If it is have you been kissed
Do you have a clue?

WHEN WONKY WOKE

The day after the night before
Actions without supervision
They can be a chore

Not controlled yet do suffer
Then the realisation
Boy – it is a Muffer!!

You danced amongst the Dandelions
Swam the deep with Seal
Yet all were acted unawares
All of it not real

When Wonky woke a wayward way
Knew in it he couldn't stay
Twisted into some strange form
Did not compute for was not the 'norm'
Wonky had to stretch to please
Had to elongate and release
The build up of the thing become
Was not Wonky as the sum

Wonky was a 'normal'
As far as 'normal' goes
Nothing much to outside stuff
Nothing much he shows

Wokey's wishes wandered
Wandering like do
Wonky maybe someone
Someone just like you

When Wonky woke it seemed a joke

CORPORATION SITUATION

Money talks and that's fact
Rich pump in and 'leaders' act
Politicians and providers
Making up the mass dividers

'look after me and I'll look after you
Those out there will have no clue
None the wiser what we do
As their lives we simply screw'

The Businesses do as please
In new ways they lead
A Corporation situation
As our 'elected' feed

Right or wrong they carry on
We are sheep to lead
Different class from that past
Fitting current breed

No-one's right without the might
Of money big and bold
Promise much but out of touch
If the truth be told

Ballot papers pick best of bad bunch
Then promises renege
Telling one thing, doing other things
The reality of the age

Not just in one Country
But across the World
Things are rearrange
To most to the absurd

A,P AFTER PUNISHMENT

Two different places suffer hard
Two different nations dealt same card
Different ways but the same
Devastation has many a name

Whilst we recover from excess
Remind ourselves we are blessed
Australia and Philippines
Know that D word – know what means

Christmas cheer and New Year
Relating to some loss, some fear
While we sit comfy in our Home
They have lost all that own

Another year turned the page
With it came nature's rage
Some do suffer, some neglect
The impact made and hell bent set

A,P Australia and Philippines
After punishment also means
Both will survive to live again
Though with one more scar
One more pain

Bless you people of these Nations
I,for one, do truly share
Maybe because my link with one
Other link so also care

SIMPLE PLEASURES
THAT I TREASURE

Me, I like Donuts
Ring or contents filled
That semi fried outer cover
Before the softness yield

The waking up each early morning
The chance to get some sleep
The wisdom that's been shared to me
The memories I keep

The travelling I've taken
The knowledge that did gain
The witnessing of those less off
The happiness and pain

Yes I am a journeyman
In more ways than one
Relishing experience
Since the day began

I am a journeyman
Since have found my Home
Different place with different face
Yet can call my own

Need I say more?

B. A.U.

Crazy flashbacks with different ending
Mental miasmas are now trending
Not Nightmares for too confusing
In retrospect almost amusing
Business as usual I suppose
As social circle grows and grows
Life events multiply
Even when we do not try

Come the 'down time' for recuperation
Come the period of restoration
Come the price of imagination
Come self imposed indignation
Then eyes snap open with confusion
All not real – just illusion
Naughty Brain with its intrusion
A waking mess am I

The world I know is falling around me
Disintegrating yet again
Brief, I know for is quite regular
Boy oh boy it's always same
Chaos rules these half baked times
Know not real but so convincing
Wobbly jelly common sense now
As an Actor is not mincing

I cannot blame it on monthly cycles
When hormones run so wild and free
For when looked again just now
Still the other, still am me
Caffeine needed in a hurry
Slap both cheeks might be good
Profanities muttered quietly
All will once again be stood

OFF MY HEAD INSTEAD

Tired feet are tweaking
Bladder close to leaking
Me I am just geeking
At some deep and complex Book
Far away from today
Lost in time for which will pay
Nothing's easy so they say
I wish more lessons took

Maybe then this so called Gem
Would make some sense to me
As it stands – more rests in hands
Is an utter mystery
How do people learn this stuff
How did Daughter for is tough
Legal shouldn't be this rough
It's supposed to help us be

Off my head instead
Of the call to go to bed
Where one can just forget instead
Then think again tomorrow
Instead Brain fed by this misled
The subject beyond my comprehension
Too long a word seems absurd
Yet none describe my sorrow

For not being smarter than the average Bear
A phrase picked up some place or time
Apt in fact for today
I am a one with one sore
Another look at this Book
Then commit it with some others
To that place where will not face
Again or ever more

MISTLETOE AND MAYBE NEXT YEAR

(Lodieta J Sumayo)

Another Christmas all alone
Far from her that holds my Heart
Getting there but still missing
Making progress so is start

Time for Family, time together
Time for reuniting, time for being one
Time for celebration
Time for having fun

Alas again not this year
Another target missed
Alas it will be in imagination
I feel that tender kiss

So Mistletoe and maybe next year
A hope that keeps me strong
A different number on Calendar
Until back where I belong

I am not that 'special' in this situation
That I truly know
Many parted from their loved ones
As world situation it does grow

Yet call me selfish if you want
For I am of myself now thinking
Thousands of miles from my new Home
As through wet eyes am blinking

Merry Christmas to one and all
Hope you can get Home
Far sooner than what started
When to birthplace I did roam

WHEN ONE ORB RISES

Sleeping time - the time of peace
Imagination is now released
Random thinking runs amok
In waking hours we can take stock

Nightmare scenario a common thing
Never knowing what will bring
Outweighed by that we think is good
More the scenario understood

In the realms of one Orb understand
In the other mischief at hand
Cannot control but just beat
With flick of arms and kick of feet

Darkness looms full of gloom
Yet through it shines a light
Daylight brings things of which sing
Things that are so bright

When one Orb rises another sets
Yet is that really true
How much of dreaming affects our thinking
In just what we do?

Subliminal classed as minimal
Yet are we right in thought
When things that 'seen' later mean
Situations in which caught

The waking hours one does savour
Full of sound, sights and flavour
Yet the self is free for interaction
When left alone with no distraction

ELECTRIC IS THE ENERGY

A Grandson's Grandson sat in bubble
Suiting up seemed so much trouble
Better to inside bring
This strange object, this strange thing
Classification embedded in forehead
Signified allowed to read
State did trust it had the power
It's own version this young one feed

Daily doses subliminally planted
Mass Mail shot extraordinaire
Yet made one crucial slip up
For in this one was thing called care
Learnt to take lessons at face value
Take them in yet not believe
For drip fed without a purpose
How does one themselves achieve

A barren wasteland outside the Bubble
Been so now for long, long time
Ancestry got too stupid
Solved dispute with technology crime
Raised an empty disaster zone
On something Nature called its own
Not no more for were the fool
Thought that we above did rule

The youngster had been to the debris
What was once called a City
There discovered in some nook
An ancient thing that they called Book
Solid learning? How fascinating
When with others integrating
Now the quandary need to ask
How come so clever their cleverness mask?

B2 6794 Alpha designation sat in bubble
Carefully peeling apart the pages
Faded but still legible
Was the stuff of ages
Not one version but of many
Different views on same thing
None to be the perfect one
For that way to now do bring

Electric is the energy
The need to say, say what be
Before consigning to forgotten - to history
The given rights of opinion free
Archived will be this simple tool
When choose to let some certain rule
Not just one for that can cope
Yet with many we lose hope

IS THE SOLUTION

Is the solution to evolution
Based on pollution and Revolution
Is the cure for being poor
Punishing and making more

Is it okay to just shrug and say
Who really cares and walk away
From it can't earn so not my concern
As another pay check freely spurn

To just walk on past without aghast
A soul who cannot remember when ate last
Is it right to adopt blinkered sight
To those Homeless on bitter night

So many questions with so many answers
Dependant upon view
Right or wrong some feel them strong
That is nothing new

Is opinion worth derision
If thought but not with act
Is something justified
Without the strength of fact

Complex conundrums to quick questions
Requiring some thought
For plain to see not all like me
In my opinion caught

EVERY NIGHT I LIE AND LIE

The things that we do tell ourselves
To help as got along
The fantasies we believe
To help us get back strong
Every night I lie and lie
In bed and to myself
Telling this broken body
Is in fact in health

Slowly it believes it
Becomes willing to just try
Though it does not speak to Heart
So knows not just why
Every night beneath the covers
I think of and miss
Two fantastic others
They keep my focused, keep me strong
Keep the reason to belong

Every day I try to play
So compos mentis I can stay
Strange I know but is my way
Not sure if I'm succeeding
Another line at a time
This wasting time is no crime
For whilst doing I feel fine
Until the time to start again

One day soon I'll be in tune
Body clock and that on wall
Until then with paper/ pen
Bit by bit I answer call
Write and write as I fight
To keep the hounds away
Hounds of the long time lonely
Waiting for a reunion

ANOTHER SHADE OF GREY

I met a friend in early morning
One I often meet
When walking in the blackness
Lit by the lights of street
The early, early time of day
When sharing with the foxes
Sharing too with old and new
Those who live with cardboard boxes

I give when can for there I am
In another life
No not each and every reason
For that cutting knife
The one that put them where they are
Outside of things we do
The Homeless are now growing
That alone is new

I see them at most vulnerable
The hours of no care
The cold, cold a.m. blanket
The bitter wind we share
I, however, am the lucky one
For I can just go back to Home
Them when it gets too cold
For warmth the roads must roam

An hour spent in this strange place
Looking at cold sad face
Of another of my Race
That has lucked out on human grace
So when will we together say
That whilst we work and play
Others slip silently away
To another shade of grey

EVERY DAY A PARADISE

The Father went out fishing
At Bank of local known
As 'Deep dirty Dunking'
As in old pictures shown
Today was no day for dunking
Today was time for talk
An afternoon and, hopefully, soon
To extent they 'walk the walk'

Father remembers what said to him
When on own journey did begin
Sage advice if truth be told
Now not the younger but the old
Same words spoken but not as token
For true they true had shown
So impart with open Heart
Now was fully grown

They said

Every day a Paradise
When do learn and then are wise
Fewer comes the big surprise
Surely, even you, think nice
The more we know the more we grow
The more within, the more can sow
'Be the Man!' let it show
Aren't afraid to say "Don't know"

The Son did look at Father
In new and quite strange way
For understood every word spoken
Absorbed what they did say

ADVANCE THE AVANT-GARDE

Everyone has a new impression
Everyone has a certain style
Everyone can make the difference
Everyone can cause a smile

Advance you of the avant-garde
It is really not that hard
Show the World what it's been missing
Whilst the money had been kissing

Go forth – Strike out you noble creatures
Display something with unknown features
Be it words or something more
There's an expanse we can explore

Be the one that now rides
The new name that then surprises
Be the next to make them think
Be the story into which they sink

Advance you brave and purposeful
Those who heard this rally call
True, I admit, not for all
Yet not worry of a fall

Go forth with vigour and belief
Go forth with skill to give relief
For the ones that need distraction
Given by interaction

Advance you of the avant-garde
Really it is not that hard
If I can do – a fool like me
Then just how hard can it be?

YOU AND ME A FANTASY

The one sat across the Table
Would be beside if able
Chose instead to use their head
So their feelings merely said
They looked into the eyes so deep
Of the partner vowed to keep
Took deep breath and said it true
What the other they did do

They simply told the truth

'You and me are fantasy
Beyond the real invention
You and me found unity
In more ways than choose to mention
We have become two parts of one
Nothing will us part
For you should know that if you go
You leave me without a Heart'

The one did sum up what had done
Since the partnership begun
The things that thought they couldn't do
The reason and who got them through
So honest said a heart it bled
As listening quite overcome
To be the thing that such feelings bring
Never thought could be that one

The couple have an almost perfect world
One I wish I had
Yet mine is fine in fact sublime
With what never thought so can't feel sad

A DIP INTO THE TREASURE TROVE

The one that felt dejected
The one that felt the pain
The one that had so much to offer
Yet reward they could not gain

The one that thought that this was 'right'
The one that was just wrong
The one that thought it was a future
Alas in they didn't belong

A dip into the Treasure trove
Memories of good times
A self inflicted punishment
For all the 'learning crimes'

The Heartbeat and despair they feel
The sense of ultimate loss
The how to cope as in sadness mope
The prize is worth the cost?

The tears and fears of no-one dear
The change then change again
The chaos of calamities
That brutal stabbing others refrain

We go through this to achieve bliss
The old pass on to young
The ones that have experienced
To those just now begun

Love and Life a strange mix
Need each other true
Yet the things both put you through
Makes wonder why we do

CALLING 'COLLECTIVES' TO CONGREGATE

Man evolved into Male and Female
Though other genders we explore
Nothing shown through skin tone
Need I say too much more?

We are all different I can relate
Yet why the need for spite and hate
This should be a one kind state
Calling 'collectives' to congregate

Apples and Pears and questioning stares
Yet both are fruit of different kind
They do fall from trees and all
Classed as Fruit you'll find

Nigerian/ Siberian
Polish and Mexican
English and Liberian
All are same and can

Disregard the differences
Concentrate on what in common
Quit disparity as insanitary
That which I hold most solemn

Calling all of intelligence
Smart enough to see the consequence
Of the pure belligerence
To enforce fictitious nonsense

SHINE ON YOU STAR ARISING

Critics and nit pickers will come aplenty
Seeking notice and jealousy
For they know that they'll never match you
Never be what they can see

Treat them as a Badge of honour
For first they must notice you
Then take time to commit their actions
All that effort to do what do

Come ascendency comes the wannabes
Come your rise come some more
Treat them as a source of humour
Come to love it even adore

Shine on you Star arising
More see you for the truth you be
Shine on you talent that's still growing
Shine and rise and so be free

THE REVOLVING EVOLUTION OF ME

I sit and think of what could have been
Think of new that have seen
Think about what now be
Think how strange reality
Ever changing - rearranging
Life a mix of highs and lows
Yet all that matters is the present
The determination that one shows

Times gone by when asked why
Now just a memory
This so strange sometimes change
The one that you now be
As long as live then can give
The best that I possess
Others things? Bring what brings
Just a new contest

The revolution in acceptance
Though with a dark and worthy side
The revolving evolution of me
A name I wear with pride
Different but not that different
Just the reasons why
All can act to adapt
If they want to try

SOMETIMES YOU SEEK

Sometimes you seek that sense so pure
Sometimes you seek to feel secure
Wrapped inside some private space
Far removed from Human Race

Sometimes you seek something more
Some adventure, again once encore
The thrill of that not tried before
Maybe on a foreign shore

Sometimes you seek an explanation
The building blocks of our creation
Curiosity may have killed the Cat
Yet not caring for that twat

Sometimes you seek that unexplained
For a challenge then have gained
A Goal, a Task, a reason why
To move on one must try

Sometimes you seek some Solitude
Though not wishing to be rude
Just some time to reflect
Make decisions then plans set

Sometimes you seek company
One or two or more than three
Some distraction the attraction
Not necessarily through interaction

Sometimes you seek and sometimes don't
Sometimes will and sometimes won't
Balanced is what seek to be
Balanced equals Harmony

Ian Wilcox

HOBBIT HURTLING HORSEBACK

Life is full of the unexpected
Life is full of unexpected things
Life is full of startling wonders
Life is full of Ropes and Strings
What 'we know' we don't really know
What we don't is often true
So we blag our way through it
If you're honest this is true

I saw a Hobbit hurtling Horseback
To where go I have no clue
For they are truly unfathomable
They just think and so then do
I never knew of their existence
Yes that's true despite my age
Then one day, hip, hip hooray
I found them courtesy of a story page

Not the normal I do grant you
In fact I guess sounds quite absurd
Yet I saw that bouncing creature
Will not repeat the things I heard!
Yet plain as day dawns seven times a week
I am sure of that for have Calendar by my side
Nothing seen quite as serene
As watching that thing try to ride!

Arms and legs akimbo
Yelps I think of joy it did employ
All can say is hope and pray
I hope it was no Boy
Each time did land upon the seat
A new menu it could eat !!

IS EVOLUTION THE SOLUTION?

When the power hungry no longer rules
When majority no longer fools
Utilising all their tools
As Humanity crumples – falls

More efficient and proficient
At sowing seeds of demise
Many more scream encore
Are we really not that wise?

Apocalypse and politics
Hand in hand it seems
Gone are days of 'people say'
Lost are future dreams

It does hurt as we revert
Then go one step more
Back to Caveman with no real plan
Then one step further sure

If not so sad I would be glad
For ironic my sense of humour
Though not comical not at all
When real becomes a rumour

On slippery slide we do glide
With one forgotten fact
Down we go but do not know
There's no mat to cushion the impact

Is evolution the solution?
When with it we move from mere tirade
When profit made by stock in trade
To bring death and world pollution

THE TEARS I CRIED

It will live with me forever
A memory etched so deep
When we first met the impression get
That you were mine to keep

The tears I cried as said Goodbye
Set in my Heart so deep
Although a man I did for can
I did truly weep

I never will forget you
You were a one so rare
You gave it all when me did call
You asked and I did dare

An experience never know before
A feeling I can't repeat
You blew me away yet couldn't stay
To join with you a feat

As I reflect know best will get
None can match you true
For am not sure could endure
The heat I felt with you

So will not another dance
At least in no way hurry
You were the best, my argument rests
You were the ultimate Curry

ADVENTURERS INTO ACCLIMATION

When from a nothing in to something
A no known to worldwide name
The pressure of the spotlights shining
All the demands that come with game

The Twenty four, seven times a week
The wish for privacy that then seek
The chance to be self again
Not just body with the name

To go to shop and not have to stop
To answer question "Is it you?"
To be able to exist stable
To in peace do what do

To live life with Husband/ Wife
Be allowed to a person be
All the glory another story
Yet neither one fits mine and me

How do those cope that live that way
How they do I cannot say
For, fortunately is not me
Nor, thank heavens, will ever be

The pitfalls of the famous
The curse of those well known
The living in the capsule
Transparent so all shown

No not for me nor family
Fortunately will never be
For have not that ambition
To be the top of tree

Ian Wilcox

CAN YOU CONVINCE

Can you convince that we are Masters
When Corn is burnt but raw inside
Can you convince me that we are Masters
When despite it all can't control the Tide

Can you convince me we are superior
When Nature works in harmony
Can you convince me that we are not interfering
In the way that things should be

We alter for our comforts
We change to make it good
Yet do we really look much further
Is our impact understood

We moan when weather turns against us
We blame everything but our self
For we are focused on one thing
Regardless we seek 'wealth'

Can you convince me that we are not changing
How things are set to be
Can you convince me that our actions
Are not borderline insanity

Easy to gloss over
Moan and groan but carry one
What topic will we moan about
When all the subjects gone?

Ian Wilcox

INSIDE ONES SELF

So many variations
So many unique creations
All in situations
As are different Nations
Yet each alone deserves a Throne
For each are King or Queen
For have done and then some
Things we haven't seen

Open eyes for the surprise
Of what does wait for you
Believe me free for I did see
What open eyes can do
The rewards are great I can state
For have them every day
The Bliss of kiss not to be missed
Nothing else to say

Those who wise have no surprise
When reading my opinion
Those who know and so grow
The seeds of one dominion

Inside ones self lies hidden wealth
Not that thing with which we pay
So much more for to adore
In who we are and what say
Forget the cover of another
Look beyond their choosing
They are not a 'job lot'
Think what might be losing

Ian Wilcox

QUESTION ASKED

'Who needs this!' one does cry
As beside a best friend die
Who on earth can say the worth
Cannot even begin to try
Watch as slow a life does go
Body parts now missing
Lips of blood not yet a flood
So gently Brother kissing

The action maybe all around
Yet not here, not this ground
For it is taken for a while
By a soldier with a smile
'Might is right so we will fight'
Said suited far from danger
Big and loud - even proud
Yet to hardship are a stranger

Easy done when for 'fun'
Commit others as a toy
Yet do bleed and sometimes need
More than you can, infact, employ
So earth nourish as blood flourish
Into a soil foreign
They answered call and gave their all
To some are not forgotten

The statistics may go ballistic
Yet of no concern to some
All they care is that we're aware
They think they're number one

Ian Wilcox

SOMEWHERE IN THE SIGNAL

Misinterpreted by that invented
Human error true
Forget about the internet
It's what we just do

Be it one on one
Looking back a twisted fun
Yet when expands to a 'Land'
Something else has just begun

Somewhere in the signal my love
We lost our conversation
Yet unlike others were not bothered
For understand the situation

Hot head led is woe instead
A thing that I abstain
Yet do not treat me as 'soft touch'
I can, when pushed, cause pain

I feel sick in even mention be
For, that in truth, is not me
Was a warrior but no more
Different path I now explore

Words are weapons yet also shield
For which other side does yield
Toss up of it's worth the cost
When in reflection see what's lost

To quote from a famous song by the awesome David Bowie
Shine on you crazy Diamond

Ian Wilcox

SUDDENLY A SUNRISE

Cool cold hours
Cool in action but are cold
The hours of the Nightshift
With so many stories told
Dark the view to a day new
The only light manmade
The Moon is hidden behind clouds
Got the worst off of the trade

Your day feels like midmorning
As just doing what you do
Talk and such to those who mean so much
Suddenly daylight from the dark breaks through
Forgotten are the hours
When others are asleep
When you try for do know why
These you aim to keep

Some a.m. and again with pen
My loved ones are busy
What to do is nothing new
Write until I feel so dizzy
No answer but a simple one
Get back to what I begun
A place upon a foreign shore
With some people I adore

Clouds are slowly clearing
If you get my meaning
The new day indeed is dawning
The radio said it's morning

WHO ARE WE THAT CLAIM TO BE?

The elder stood at tribal gathering
An old custom in new age
In the lore of its history
This could be seen as new page

Well known for their wisdom
Mixing sugar with the spice
All to them did listen
When imparting some advice

Leaned on stick half wrist thick
Took a breath and spoke
What did say with words that play?
Were serious, not some joke

Had watched the world as it unfurled
Into something quite unknown
Lost its way some might say
In the actions shown

Technology was meant to be
An aid and not to rule
Yet we became that pawn in name
No better than the fool

We did not mix so couldn't fix
The disparities of culture
We then bled as modern led
Whilst looked on the Vulture

Who are we to claim to be?
The knowing while not showing
The cause for pause when claims adores
This world in which we grow?

HARMONIES A MYSTERY

Paano ko sisimulan na sabihin sa iyo kung gaano kita kamahal?

I came out of curiosity
Found the one that with want to be
Magic stirred and was heard
Results are plain to see

Been the single then senses tingle
A new way was so found
The sensation in acclimatisation
I broadcast and astound

The one begun the 'simple bum'
Grew and so did change
Life it took another look
Gave, until then, so strange

Harmonies a mystery
Yet when find are so worthwhile
Started as a simple word
A brief but magic smile

What more for sure can one explore
Apart from the joy that's found
When find the other half of kind
When meet on common ground

Love you lots my Darling
Love what you gave to me
Love you for still giving
Love with every part of me

NOTHING REALLY MATTERS

Life it sucked in the Farmyard
Produce until did die
Many questions to be asked
With no true answer why

Life it sucks in the workplace
Never fitting in
Too insecure to be 'real pure'
The socialising sin

All aghast because of past
A deep routed memory
Of what seen and did mean
The other chance to be

All been through was something new
Education is salvation
Live and learn to a future earn
Beast and every Nation

"Nothing really matters"
So said the Wren to Hen
"Nothing strange when have to change
Have to think to begin again"

So nothing really matters
Apart from how you act
Think is drink and not much more
Progression an impact

Been and don't and wear the scars
Scars are not today
Just a thing that past once bring
So let future have its say

Ian Wilcox

SO WHAT IS SUNSET

The world gets smaller everyday
We can now see as well as say
We talk in 'zones' not our own
Yet with still serious and some play

Each has time and that time's fine
For you as well need structure
Then employ the global toy
Thinking now a clutter

Add to this the kiss I miss
Conception is much more
To understand that cannot hold the hand
Of the one who I adore

So what is Sunset when can't see
What it looks like away from me
What is the end of day
When I am still so far away?

Time goes slow so far from Home
In oneself not real
It's about what you want
About feelings that you feel

I love my love and am not proud
That I declare them both out loud
The one who, through care, made me
The one who will achieve what cannot be

Met one and Three become
The story of the strange
For I was until the time
My future did rearrange

Memories fast and things don't last
Just the click of time
Soon will go this time so slow
Until again I hold divine

Wistful is just blissful
The Truth a bitter pill
Yet with hope I can still cope
The power of the Will!

THE MAN A KIN

Repetitive is taxing
When achieving becoming pain
Just more bore if 'like' not sure
So little felt to gain
Had promised much so as such
Must breathe and then deliver
Even though it doesn't show
Hand shakes and lips do quiver

The man was now so undecided
Sat on fence so much became a part
The man a kin to Mannequin
So troubled was his art
The 'block' they said to empty Head
As searching what to do
So much done missing the fun
Of creating something new

Once more the lure of distant shore
Overriding in their thoughts
The reason why they must try
For in expression caught
The musings quite confusing
The result of which uncertain
As feed the need to tap with speed
The keys early behind closed Curtains

Another done that was not fun
In the comical sense at least
Just more ink to on page sink
For other eyes to feast

WANDERING WISTFULLY
WITHOUT SUNLIGHT

Sometimes you need a moment
Sometimes you need some space
Sometimes want some solitude
Away from that you face

When attraction becomes distraction
Something else is sought
A breakaway from crazy day
Before in another caught

So the time just feels fine
Shared with the unspoken, but not few
Moon and electric light, now new bulbs and so, so bright
An option that can do

The beautiful peace of the release
The comfort within the solitude
Not much chance of hateful glance
Of day walkers sometimes rude

Sharing streets with natures feats
The nocturnal that slip by
No conversation for from different nations
Understanding so know why

Preparing for the sharing
Of those yet to awake
Wandering wistfully without sunlight
A chance one likes to take

SHIFT THE SHITE

Hey you out there! Have a care
We don't want to see your woes
We all grow as things go
Not each experience on FB shows

Nothing great nor relate
To minor trifles needing attention
Nor give fig of what consider big
When have had some I can't mention

Attention seeking and 'Heart leaking'
Not the thing I choose
Constant use is abuse
Of a personality whose strength is loose

Write about 'lost love' sure
Just about and nothing more
Not about how hard it is
When you sit in health's kiss

Drama is for the Actors
Containing reason amongst its factors
Not some type of chance to see
Someone saying 'Woe is me'

If can find time to say that luck's gone away
Then why not say that you are strong?
Why not instead tell how it led
To knowing that life's not just song

Hey yah you read and do
Open eyes and see
You are you and can do
Possibility is a thing that's free

'CRYSTALLISED' IN CHARACTER

The Archaeologists dug and scraped
A 'new finding' hoped to make
The things they found did astound
New grounds in understanding break

We all gained wisdom from their works

A History that's new to me
A chance to see what could not see
A past experience of 'Family'
In the Human progress tree

Progress is a fascination

Archaeology and ancestry
What a pleasure to find treasure
Mixed with shock in equal measure
Not a record to be taken at leisure

Live and learn so hope we live

Some rules of fools created tools
Not for good but harm
To invade instead of trade
No wish to just charm

Now look at where we are now?

Crystallised in character
Nothing much seems to matter
As personal we choose to scatter
The reap before the sow

MEANWHILE IN SOME UNKNOWN PLACE

Sunday's such a bloody pain
So much so I must refrain
From expletives want to use
When limited time in which to choose
Fast food or some such stuff
This 'Sunday trading' makes life tough

Meanwhile in some unknown place
Someone searching for what can eat
Rocks and various other objects
Cut and bruise their bare feet

Why don't shops open same
Each other has day within its name
Why am I restricted to when can buy
For some stupid reason why
The rules today are so bizarre
In the age of electronic car

Meanwhile in some unknown place
A four mile walk to get a drink
That of water – nothing more
Not the luxury of it from sink

Nearly midday so at last
Can get some one else to cook
Just need now to endure the hassle
Of by phone I have to book
This life is trying at it's best
More so on this 'day of rest'

Meanwhile in some unknown place
Someone dies of malnutrition
Not their fault just how goes
When just living is a mission

IF NO~ONE CARED

If no-one dared and no-one shared
If no-one cared and no-one 'aired'
If no-one gave a toss
What would be the thing we see
What would be the loss?

If just for self and gained 'wealth'
If just for one we become
If solitary we choose to be
If each becomes own nationality
What would be the future?

A question asked as a task
To contemplate at rest
When I find that my own Mind
Does its thinking best

How a world so absurd
How did get to this
How can change something strange
Defying Reapers kiss?

Why do I try to not just cry
Why am I this now writing
Why is calming in the action
Why do find it frightening?

Alas don't know so have to go
Alas no answer give
Alas it will take much change
Alas still have to live

SEEN FROM SOCRATES

Seen some things and took on-board
So much stuff misunderstood
Parenting and adulthood
Then we get the bad and good

Lack of skills an epidemic
When not shown as growing up
Exasperate a basic problem
When main concern is Wi-Fi shut

Ancient times things were clearer
At least is my point of view
Had their bad points I admit
Though nothing like compared to new

Now producing new breed reliant
On something else to do their thinking
Tapping at some devices
Whilst a Coffee House drink drinking

'Who am I?
I am successful
Making money
So forgetful'

The repeated message
Send our self
Pause a moment
Is this Health?

Seen from Socrates a way showing
The beauty of a Mind that's growing
The need for and then sowing
The treasury of all the knowing

AS A TOKEN

Softly spoken as a token
No wish for confrontation
Merely cause for a pause
In some heated situations

Softly spoken as a token
To express your care
Personal so just one knows
In a place no wish to share

Softly spoken so can relate
Not a lecture but educate
No criticism was this thing
Just experience choose to bring

When escalation of situation
Is last thing that was your choice
Low volume words to one just heard
Said with quiet noice

When emphasise to cut with knife
Soft just makes impact
Not outburst that's incurred
A precursor to an act

Softly spoken as wish to teach
Not criticise nor beseech
Just passing on from things have done
No scolding just surprise

IN MY BLOOD

'Horace' in the blood
As the words they flood
Head to pen and then again
The beauty of the word
So long ago yet still know
The craft they made so famous
Their work is etched into History
Their legend quite contagious

Many Arts with past starts
We just take for granted
Yet with the new of their brew
We become enchanted
New styles fine and sometimes sublime
Yet just how much each does know
Of the ones who becomes
A classroom type of show

In my blood like Fatherhood
The ability to write
Not just form that's now so norm
To give to some insight
The ability to educate
The ability to relate
The ability to not dictate
The ability to cause a smile

Horace a shorter name
For a great and talented Man
Of ancient Rome who is known
Who said because they ran
Not in the normal sense of word
They ran with the thought
Put them down so we can
Be better when we taught

THOSE MORNING LEGS

'Chicken run' is such fun
As stretched those morning legs
Unlock door just after Four
Then gather up some Eggs

No neck break for goodness sake
A factory in the living
Why destroy those who employ
And are freely giving

The stretch of muscle and hair tussle
The breaking of the sleep
First foot awkward as recorded
Horizontal wish to keep

Body keen for Caffeine
The kick-start to the next
The 'all knowing' and is showing
It's somewhat perplexed

Aching limbs but big grins
Another shift complete
For those who do (and not a few)
Walk the dark strange street

Two or Four or legs more
Unseen by most of us
Suits them fine for not is crime
When in seeing they don't trust

Those morning legs, those ole pegs
How many the repeat
More! Encore! I implore
Never please retreat

SOMETHING STRANGE
SO HAD TO CHANGE

Red and Green should not be seen
Together on a wall
So was told as both did hold
Guess will make the return call
Nah, I like the combination

Pork and pickle something fickle
According to the 'expert taste'
Too late now to change to cow
No sense to it just waste
Wow! - it's delicious!!!

Have to act to attract
Not my thing you see
Get what seen so that does mean
What you saw was me
Up to you after that

Apparently a brain's that's free
Not welcome by some fools
Like to indoctrinate to their state
With some hideous developed tools
Best of luck sucker

Something strange so had to change
Though no harm it would cause
So before do I think it's new
Then I take a pause
I am just me and nothing else

THE MIRROR CRACKED

The mirror cracked as hatred spat
Across a world so small
The mirror broke as personal spoke
Instead of for us all
The anger was a dangerous thing
The impact of what could bring
Not the harmony of which should sing
This was purely vile

The mirror broke for no joke
The reflection not unfit
Just needed change from something strange
Just a little bit
What knew before now no more
The old seem to have lost
The new grew as 'what through'
The question "at what cost?"

Some changes good is understood
When lead to understanding
Yet some not when all got
Some 'brainwash' that they are handing
They more implore you to adore
Then their wishes do
Yet they are above that act itself
Sadly nothing new

Beware the cracked glass my friend
Ask the reason why
Do not accept that of Hate
When you can Love instead try

TIME IS

What is time to you?
What with it will you do
Something old or something new
What is time for you?

Time for me is everything
Precious valuable for everyone
Time is not to be wasted
Time oh time is equal to everyone

How you use it is differ
Time is not controllable
And if not used at the right time,
It will cause problems to the person using it,
No one can reverse it,

When it gone, gone forever
Never to be seen again
That's why they say
Time waits for no one

Time is an element that if it changed by just 1%
If will affect everything

Plants, humans, food
Darkness, light, everything will be wrong without time.
Our time must be spent wisely

Profitable things for our time
Time wasted can never be regained
Use your time and make the best of it,
To profit yourself and others.

What is Time but 'tick tock'
Sweeping hands of the clock
Maybe staggered as designed
The fact they tell no time of mine

What is time to you my Sis?
Do you wish for or just miss?
What is time when no perception
What is time in reflection?

What say you - please a clue
For the actual merely reality
Nothing for the things we think
Nothing to that we do see

Bose Enduwe Adogah and Ian Wilcox

VERIFICATION IN THE VERNACULAR

Verification in the vernacular is something quite spectacular
Different places, different people
The multitude is daunting
Yet get past that initial blast
Becomes a thing less haunting
To know is grow and now so
I reason to try to learn
For by that which swallowed not spat
Broader friends you earn

With languages and dialects
When encounter and then inspect
A greater understanding get
That we are all the same
Like food good that's understood
Spoken is a treat
When understand from another Land
A certain bonding now complete

The more can show in someway know
The better you become
For we are not such diversity
We are all but one

WITH FULCRUM
FOR A FUTURE

Had enough of struggling
Inner and outer pair
Was not happy with the person
Who returns my stare

Not much fun being glum
Time to make a change
Let's see what gives positive
Enjoyable but strange

With fulcrum for a future sat
Done the past – enough of that
Moving balance to then go
To a better place I know

Yes I did and found that hid
A whole new way to be
Got attention from reflection
That really is uncanny

Not much changed but everything
Just changed the old down me
Found a different Mister
That Mister calm now be

Growing up is just luck
A lottery it's true
Then there comes an important choice
'What now do I do?'

'FAST' OR 'FITNESS'

'Fast' or 'Fitness' understood
Yet should be at times when to you are good
Everything in some moderation
For depending upon situation
Sometimes you just need a tummy fill
Sometimes you can exert your will
Home a place that you can choose
Work a place you sometimes lose

Convenience is not so bad
When all is could have or had
Now the chains have rearranged
Now their menus somewhat changed
Yes, they are still 'fast food'
Sometimes had when in the mood
Could not be bothered to something take
We are all humans for goodness sake!

Everything in moderation
The perfect answer to the equation
Dependent on the situation
Just use your head and choose

'KILLING' ONESELF
IN COMFORT

Changing zones to not your own
For the chance to speak and see
Those who you hold so close
Where you wish to be

Matching them with what have
A long day does ensure
Yet the worth my seem absurd
It is the perfect cure

Killing oneself through lack of sleep
Sleep can be recovered
Not the wish to somehow kiss
The lips of more than other

Gladly willing if is killing
For opposite is worse
The part of heart when apart
A simple timing curse

WHY ONE DAY?

(Inspirited by David Bowie)

As a great artist sang and said
Words so deeply etched in head
Resonates without sound
For a message so profound
'We can be Heroes for one day'
Were part of words that one did say
Why a day and not much more
Why not something so much more?

Be a Hero or Heroine
First we must just begin
Not, necessarily, one to all
Just to those we children call
Be the one who they respect
Be the standard want to get
If nothing else you can give
Part to them a way to live

Why one day and not now
Why not just a simple clue
Why not start to impart
All the things should don't and do
None of us are perfect
None will ever be
Just try to be a good Parent
Tell what you did see

Ian Wilcox

Lightning Source UK Ltd.
Milton Keynes UK
UKHW011940060821
388460UK00008B/546/J